This story is pa...
To aid your ...
to some of the ...

A&E (Accident & ...

Community Midw... ...
with specialist training in midwifery, or the delivery
of infants.

Health visitor—a nurse trained in preventative
medicine and midwifery, who educates people
caring for dependants, e.g babies or the elderly.

House officer—a hospital-based trainee doctor;
also known as an intern or resident.

ITU—Intensive Therapy Unit; a hospital department
where intensive care is given to those patients in a
critical condition or after major operations.

Locum—a doctor who temporarily stands in for
another, due to absence or illness.

NHS—National Health Service; the U.K. public health
system, which offers medical and surgical care, and is
funded by taxpayers.

Obstetrician—a medical professional specializing in
the care of women during pregnancy, labor and the
period immediately after the birth.

Consultant—a senior medical professional
specializing in an area of medicine.

Senior registrar—a specialist surgeon or doctor
who is subordinate to a consultant, but senior to
the house officers.

SHO—senior house officer—after registration, a
doctor who continues working in a hospital can
be appointed to this full-time, training position.

INTERNATIONAL
DOCTORS

They're guaranteed to raise your pulse!

Meet the most eligible medical men of the
world, in a new series of stories by popular
authors that will make your heart race!

Whether they're saving lives or curing your
desire, our doctors have got bedside manners
that send temperatures soaring....

Look for more heart-stopping titles
in this ongoing new series.

Available only from Harlequin Presents®.

Sarah Morgan

THE DOCTOR'S RUNAWAY BRIDE

INTERNATIONAL
DOCTORS

HARLEQUIN®

TORONTO • NEW YORK • LONDON
AMSTERDAM • PARIS • SYDNEY • HAMBURG
STOCKHOLM • ATHENS • TOKYO • MILAN • MADRID
PRAGUE • WARSAW • BUDAPEST • AUCKLAND

To Suzy

For your encouragement, expertise and humor, and for being the best editor a girl could have.

ISBN 0-373-12366-3

THE DOCTOR'S RUNAWAY BRIDE

First North American Publication 2003.

This edition published by arrangement with Harlequin Books S.A.

Visit us at www.eHarlequin.com

Printed in U.S.A.

PROLOGUE

'*I CAN'T* marry him.'

Pale and shaking, Tia Franklin struggled with the zip of her sleek white wedding dress, sobbing with frustration when it stubbornly refused to budge.

'Tia, wait—you'll tear it—' Sharon, her best friend and bridesmaid, tried frantically to calm her down but Tia wasn't taking any notice.

'I don't care.' As if to prove her point, Tia jerked at the zip again, her sobs increasing as it jammed and the material ripped. 'What does it matter? I'm not getting married now, so I certainly don't need a dress.'

Sharon stood still, frozen with horror. 'Tia, the wedding starts in half an hour and there are one hundred and forty guests waiting in the church—'

'I don't care about that, either.' Tia finally managed to wriggle out of the dress and stumbled across the hotel room to her suitcase, which was already packed for her honeymoon.

She released the catch and grabbed the first outfit that came to hand, tears falling steadily down her cheeks as she struggled into a pair of silk trousers and matching jacket.

Sharon was still staring at her, open-mouthed with disbelief. 'What's happened? You were so happy—and no wonder. Luca Zattoni is every woman's fantasy. Rich, cool-headed, Italian, body to die for...'

Despite her tears, Tia lifted an eyebrow. 'I thought you were a happily married woman?'

'I am.' Sharon looked unrepentant. 'But there isn't a woman alive who wouldn't look twice at Luca. He's sex on legs, Tia.'

Sex on legs.

Tia felt her heart beat faster. And that was the reason for the current mess. She hadn't been able to resist the man.

Sharon sighed. 'Tia, the entire female population is green with envy. You're the one that he's marrying.'

Tia lifted her chin. 'Not any more.'

Thoroughly alarmed, Sharon bustled across to her friend and took her by the shoulders. 'OK, calm down. Take a deep breath. Copy me…' She breathed slowly, trying to set an example. 'Right. That's better. Now, then, tell me slowly, has something happened or is this just bridal nerves? I was nervous before I married Richard, you know. It's normal to be nervous. Especially for someone with your background.'

'It's not nerves.' Tia pulled away from her friend and rammed her feet into the first pair of shoes that came to hand.

Totally at a loss, Sharon backed away and turned towards the door. 'I'll fetch Luca.'

Dear God, no! That was the last thing she wanted.

'I don't want to see Luca!' Tia's head jerked up and the desperation in her voice stopped Sharon in her tracks. 'I can't. I just want to get out of here as fast as possible.'

'Tia…' Sharon let go of the doorhandle and tried to reason with her, her voice soothing. 'Just because things didn't work out for your parents, it doesn't mean—'

'What?' Tia slammed the suitcase shut and stared at her, tendrils of blonde hair escaping from what had once been an elegant chignon. 'What doesn't it mean? That it will all go wrong for me, too? My mother drank herself into the grave because she discovered that the man she loved—*the man she trusted*—had betrayed her. Kept secrets from her. Do you really think I intend to put myself in the same position?'

Clamping her teeth onto her lower lip, Tia walked back

across the room and swept her make-up off the dressing-table into her handbag.

'I don't understand.' Sharon looked blank. 'I know that your father had affairs, but—' She broke off, her eyes widening as she registered what Tia had just said. 'Are you saying that you think Luca is *having an affair*?'

Tia felt the pain, hot and fluid, pour along her veins.

'I don't know,' she said honestly. 'I think so. Maybe. He's certainly having a serious relationship with another woman.'

'No.' Sharon shook her head and gave an incredulous laugh. 'No! I don't believe it. I never saw a man more in love with a woman than Luca is with you. He's crazy about you.'

Tia closed her eyes and took steadying breaths.

If only…

'Trust me on this one, Sharon,' she said finally. 'Luca is not in love with me.'

'So, if he doesn't love you, why are there one hundred and forty people waiting for you to marry him, and why am I dressed like a green blancmange?'

There was a long silence and when Tia finally spoke her voice was little more than a hoarse croak.

'Because I'm pregnant.'

The room was suddenly deadly quiet. 'Tia?'

'That's the reason he's marrying me.' Tia gave a wobbly smile and blushed deeply. 'And before you say it, yes, I'm a midwife and I should know the facts of life, but somehow I forgot them when I met Luca.'

In fact, she'd forgotten pretty much everything the moment she'd set eyes on Luca.

Fundamental things like how to walk away from a man before things became serious.

The truth was that Luca Zattoni was the most overwhelmingly attractive male she'd ever met. Cool and confident and stunningly good-looking, the chemistry between them had stopped her brain from functioning from the moment they'd met.

And that moment was etched in her memory for ever.

She'd been backpacking around Europe and she'd arrived in Venice late at night. As she'd left the bus station, a group of young lads had started to bother her and she'd felt a rush of relief when a car had suddenly pulled up.

Luca had stepped out of the driver's seat, broad-shouldered and menacing as he'd strode towards the youths who had surrounded her, his glossy hair shining blue-black under the streetlamps. He was clearly a man who could handle himself in any situation and her tormenters had melted rapidly into the darkness, leaving the two of them alone.

So she'd been left standing next to an empty bus station, awkwardly muttering her thanks to this handsome Italian stranger whose dark-eyed scrutiny had made her feel decidedly light headed.

'It's late to be wandering the streets of Venice,' he observed, his gaze flickering over her backpack and resting on her sturdy walking boots. 'Can I give you a lift somewhere?'

He spoke in English and he had the sexiest voice she'd ever heard. Smooth, masculine tones tinged with enough of an Italian accent to make the blood heat in her veins.

Tia's heart was thumping so hard she thought it might burst through her ribcage. 'H-how did you guess that I'm English?'

'Not difficult.' His eyes rested briefly on her silver blonde hair and he gave her a smile that made her breathing stop. 'Hair the colour of yours is very unusual in Italy. As you will discover if you continue to walk the streets at this time of night.'

She was still staring at him like an idiot. 'I haven't found anywhere to stay yet...'

'Venice is generally a very safe city,' he told her, 'but a

woman like you shouldn't be walking around on her own this late.'

A woman like her...

Her eyes locked with his and something passed between them. A feeling so powerful that her knees weakened alarmingly.

His eyes held hers captive, drawing her in. 'I would be happy to show you around and help you find somewhere to stay...'

She knew that getting into a car with a stranger was foolish in the extreme, but this man didn't seem like a stranger and their relationship progressed so fast she barely had time to reason.

And then Tia discovered that she was pregnant.

She dragged herself back to the present, aware that Sharon was still staring at her, clearly taken aback by her announcement.

'And you think that's why he's marrying you?'

'I didn't at first.' Tia's voice shook as she told Sharon what had happened. 'I believed what I wanted to believe—that he loved me and that was why he was marrying me.'

Sharon bit her lip. 'So...'

Tia took a deep breath. 'But I've found out that he was just using me as therapy. It seems he was getting over another relationship.' She shook her head slowly as she thought back over the past few weeks. 'He only proposed because I told him I was pregnant.'

Sharon looked horrified. 'How—? What makes you think he's involved with someone else?'

'Because I just met her.' Tia dropped the bag and stared into the mirror. Her reflection stared back, her skin pale and streaked with tears. 'I nipped along the corridor to talk to Luca's mother half an hour ago, when you were in the bathroom. She was deep in conversation with a very stunning woman. Someone I'd never seen before.'

Sharon sank onto the nearest chair and stared at her with trepidation. 'And?'

Tia fiddled with the silk of her jacket. 'His mother was saying what a sad day it was. That he should have been marrying Luisa—that's her name, by the way.' She sniffed slightly. 'And that he was marrying totally the wrong woman for totally the wrong reasons and it would never last.'

Sharon gave a soft gasp and lifted a hand to her throat. 'And what did this Luisa woman say?'

'That she and Luca had been so close for so long that things had just become confused. And that she'd seen him and spoken to him and he'd said he would always love her…'

'No!' Sharon groaned and shook her head. 'I don't believe it. Not Luca.'

Tia gave her a watery smile. 'Why not Luca? Let's be honest for a moment. This has been one of the fastest romances on record. I met him ten weeks ago. We barely know him, Shaz.' Tia's voice cracked and Sharon squeezed her arm.

'Luca's not a teenager, Tia. He's an adult male who knows exactly what he wants out of life. I can't see him marrying someone unless he wanted to. Maybe he finished it—'

'No.' Tia rummaged in her bag for a tissue and blew her nose hard. 'No way would any red-blooded male finish with a woman like this one. You didn't see her. She was seriously gorgeous. And elegant. Nothing like me. When Luca met me I was backpacking, for goodness' sake! I'm so far removed from his usual style of woman that it's laughable. I'm a homeless, rootless waif who's terrified of commitment. Believe me, there's no contest.'

Sharon frowned. 'You forgot to add that you're also warm, funny and irresistibly pretty. Tia, men have been falling over themselves to get to you for years and you don't even see it. Trust me, Luca is crazy about you—'

'Novelty value.' Tia blew her nose again and tucked the tissue up her sleeve. 'There's obviously a shortage of blonde women in Italy. But I've come to my senses now, and I'm relieving him of his responsibilities. He can go back to the woman he loves. Come to think of it, he's probably never been away from her. Maybe that's why he was spending all that time at the hospital.'

'He's an obstetrician.' Sharon reasoned. 'You know they work hideous hours.'

'Do I?'

What evidence did she have that he'd been working? Only his word, and he seemed to be very selective about what he disclosed.

And she could never marry a man who wasn't completely honest with her.

She stood up, slipped on her coat and picked up her bags.

'Tia, wait!' Sharon hastily followed her across the room and caught her arm. 'At least talk to Luca about it before you leave. There might be a simple explanation.'

Tia shook her head. 'For telling another woman that he would always love her? I don't think so.'

'But—'

'He doesn't love me, Shaz. He was just doing the honourable thing by offering to marry me and I was really stupid to believe otherwise.'

Luca had never once said he loved her. Not even when she'd told him about the baby and he'd proposed.

Sometimes, just sometimes, from the way he'd behaved, she'd thought that maybe—

But she'd just been kidding herself.

'He doesn't love me.' Tia moved towards the door and Sharon grabbed her again.

'He's going to be furious, Tia.'

Tia shook her head slowly. 'I don't think so.' She gave

a painful smile. 'I think he'll be relieved that I've let him off the hook.'

Sharon looked at her anxiously. 'So what are you going to do?'

Tia checked that her passport was in her handbag. 'Take the first available flight back to England. With any luck you'll give me my old job back and I'll find somewhere to live…'

Sharon frowned. 'Of course you can have your job back, and you can stay with Richard and me, but—'

'No. I need to be on my own.'

Sharon bit her lip. 'But, Tia, Luca is a very traditional Italian male. Do you really think he's going to let you leave, knowing you're pregnant? He'll follow you—'

'No.' Tia gave a sad smile and shook her head. 'If we were already married, then maybe, but Luca is still a single man and he's free to lead his own life.'

Free to marry Luisa.

'It's over, Shaz, and I need to build a new life for myself.'

Without Luca.

CHAPTER ONE

SHE wasn't going to cry.

Tia clamped her teeth firmly on her lower lip and wondered if the day would ever come when she no longer felt like sobbing the whole time.

A soft sigh from the newly delivered mother by her side brought her to her senses and she stared down at the tiny bundle in her arms.

The child was beautiful.

Barely two hours old, dark lashes feathered her cheeks which were still slightly blotched from the rigours of birth. Lying passively in Tia's arms, she gazed placidly up at the world, her blue eyes slightly unfocused.

Tia felt her throat close.

'Isn't she perfect?' The proud mother gave a wide, self-satisfied smile and waited to be handed her daughter. 'I can't believe how beautiful she is. I mean, I always thought babies were supposed to be ugly.'

Ugly?

Tia stared down at the sleeping cherub, marvelling at the way nature had managed to produce everything in miniature.

No—the baby definitely wasn't ugly.

'She's beautiful, Mrs Adams.' Tia's heart beat faster as the baby made little snuffly noises and turned her head searchingly. 'And she's hungry.'

Work. Thank goodness for work. It was the only thing that distracted her from her own problems.

She tightened the blanket around the baby and looked quizzically at Fiona Adams. 'Are you ready to give it a try?'

'I suppose so, although I have to admit that I'm really nervous,' the young woman admitted as she settled herself more comfortably on the chair. 'Everyone says I'm mad, wanting to breastfeed.'

'You're not mad at all,' Tia said calmly. 'Breast milk is designed for babies and you're giving her the very best start in life.'

Fiona looked worried. 'I bet I won't have enough milk.'

'Well, your milk often doesn't come in for a few days after delivery,' Tia told her, 'but what you do produce is something called colostrum.'

'And that's good for her?'

Tia nodded. 'Very good for her. Packed full of protein and antibodies. Very high in calories, too. Are you comfortable like that?'

She'd settled Fiona in a chair with her back and her feet supported.

Fiona wriggled again and held out her arms. 'Yes. I really wanted to put her straight on the breast after she was delivered, but she was totally out for the count.'

Tia nodded. 'You had pethidine during your labour, and it can make the baby sleepy.' She placed the baby in Fiona's arms, positioning her carefully. 'That's right. We want her mouth to be opposite the nipple, just like that—perfect.'

Fiona stared down at her baby daughter. 'Does the position really matter?'

'Oh, yes. It's vital if you're not going to get sore and disheartened by the whole thing. Everyone thinks that breastfeeding is instinctive, but it isn't, you know.' Her voice was soft as she tucked the baby into a good position, moving Fiona's arm so that she supported the baby's shoulders. 'It's a skill that has to be learned like any other. That's great, Fiona. You can use your fingers to support her head—like that. Brilliant.'

She slipped a hand behind the baby's downy head and

gently moved the baby's mouth against the nipple, encouraging her to suck. 'Come on, sweetheart, take a nice big mouthful for me...'

'Oh!' Fiona breathed in sharply and then looked up, her eyes misty. 'She's doing it! I can feel it.'

'That's great.' Tia watched the baby closely, checking that she was sucking properly. 'You're both doing really well.'

'So is that it? I expected it to be more complicated than that.'

Tia smiled. 'Well, sometimes it is. And for the first few days it's a good idea to let someone help you put her on the breast so that we can check that she's feeding properly.'

Fiona stared down at her daughter with an awed expression in her eyes. 'I can't believe that it doesn't hurt. I always expected it to.'

Tia shook her head. 'It shouldn't hurt. Not if she's latched on properly.'

'And how do I know that?'

'Well, for a start there shouldn't be any pain,' Tia said, 'and also if you look down you can see that she's taken the whole of the nipple and some of the breast into her mouth. That's how it works, you see. The nipple goes right back as far as the soft palate and that's what makes her suck. Her lower jaw closes on the actual breast tissue and she uses suction to strip the breast of milk. You'll feel her feeding but it should never be painful.'

'And what if I can't make enough milk?'

Tia gave a lopsided smile. 'Well, that's where nature is very clever. It's all about supply and demand. The more you put the baby to the breast, the more milk you produce.'

Fiona gave a contented sigh and settled down to enjoy feeding her daughter.

'You have a very unusual name.' She glanced up at Tia with a curious smile. 'What's its origin?'

Tia pulled a face. 'It's short for Portia.'

Fiona lifted her eyebrows. 'As in *The Merchant of Venice*?'

Tia gave a nod and a rueful smile. 'My parents were actors.'

'It's a pretty name,' Fiona commented, breaking off as her husband walked into the room, a bag of coins and a sheet of paper clasped in his hand.

'Mike, look!' Fiona spoke softly so that she didn't disturb the baby. 'She's feeding!'

Mike Adams flopped onto the bed and grinned soppily at his wife. 'Clever girl. I knew you could do it.'

'It's her that's doing it, not me.' Fiona touched her daughter's downy head with her fingers. 'She's brilliant.'

'She knows what's good for her,' Mike said stoutly, and Fiona gave him a wry look.

'And you, too, of course. You can't get up in the night if I'm breastfeeding.'

'Oops. Caught out!' Mike smiled sheepishly. 'I'll do the nappies.'

Fiona smiled placidly. 'Too right you will. And the winding.' She frowned at her husband. 'You look really rumpled. As if you slept in your clothes.'

Mike gave a short laugh. 'Sleep? Just remind me what that is again. You may have been the one who had the baby, but I'm exhausted!'

'Poor thing!' Fiona laughed. 'So, who did you phone?'

Mike gave a groan and ticked them off on his fingers. 'Your mother, my mother, your sister, Pam and Rick, Sue and Simon and Nick Whiteshaw.'

'Oh, great, well done.' Fiona turned her attention back to the baby and then glanced at Tia. 'How long do I keep going for?'

'Until she stops feeding.' Tia gazed down at the baby, noticing that she was still swallowing. 'She's still guzzling away at the moment.'

'Do I have to give her both sides?'

'Always offer both sides,' Tia advised. 'But let her take all that she wants to from the first breast. When your milk comes in it's important that she stays on the breast for as long as she wants to because the milk changes during the feed.'

Fiona's eyes widened. 'Really?'

'Really.' Tia smiled. 'What the baby gets first is what we call foremilk—it's lower in calories and thirst-quenching. After that they drink hind milk which is much more filling. If you take them off the breast too soon then they miss out on the milk that fills them up.'

Mike blinked. 'Clever.'

'Very.' Tia nodded and helped Fiona remove the sleepy baby from her breast and wind her carefully. 'Have you decided on a name yet?'

'We've narrowed it down to three,' Fiona said with a chuckle. 'Mike's first choice is Georgia, mine is Isabelle and we both quite like Megan.'

'Megan Adams.' Tia tried it out, nodded her approval and took the baby from Fiona, snuggling her against her shoulder with an easy confidence that brought an envious sigh from the mother.

'You're so natural with her. Do you have children?'

'No.'

Not yet…

Suddenly Tia needed some air. She placed the baby carefully in the cot and drew the curtains back round the bed. 'Give me a shout next time she's ready to feed and I'll help you, Fiona.'

Forcing a smile, she hurried out of the four-bedded bay and back to the nurses' station, taking a long, steadying breath as she tentatively touched her still flat stomach.

Her heart stumbled and panic swamped her.

This wasn't the way things should have turned out.

She'd never wanted to bring a baby into the world on

her own. After her own experiences it was the last thing she would have wished on a child.

Taking a deep breath, she forced herself to think rationally. She'd cope, of course she would. Plenty of people did. Not everyone was like her own mother and there was no reason why she should be, but still…

Dragging her mind back to her work, she settled herself at the computer and updated Fiona's notes, glancing up as Sharon, in full professional mode as the unit sister, bustled up to the nurses' station.

'Are you still here, Tia?' She frowned and checked the clock on the wall. 'You should have gone home hours ago.'

Tia ignored her.

She didn't want to go home. She liked being at work. It took her mind off her problems.

'Baby Adams has taken her first feed nicely,' she told Sharon, her smile overly bright. 'I'm just updating the notes and then I'll go and check on Mrs Dodd if you like.'

'What I'd like is for you to stop pretending nothing is wrong.' Sharon lowered her voice and glanced up the corridor to check that no one was within earshot. 'Have you called him?'

'No.' Tia turned back to the computer, vaguely registering that Sharon looked slightly agitated about something. 'And I don't intend to.'

'But if he comes to you, you'd talk to him?'

'Sharon, I left the man standing at the altar,' Tia reminded her patiently, wondering why her friend was looking so nervous, 'and he's in love with another woman. There's no earthly reason why he would possibly want to see me ever again.'

'Except, maybe, that you're carrying his child,' Sharon pointed out quietly, her eyes flickering briefly down to Tia's flat stomach. 'Talking of which, how are you?'

Tia pulled a face. 'Oh, you know, sick, exhausted—apart from that, fine.'

Sharon didn't smile. 'You need to register with a doctor, Tia.'

Tia nodded and didn't meet her eyes. 'Plenty of time for that.' Not wanting to pursue the topic, she stood up and tucked her notebook into her pocket. 'Maybe you're right about it being time to go home. I'll see you tomorrow.'

Sharon looked suddenly flustered. 'Tia, wait, there's something I—'

'Not now, Sharon.' Tia interrupted her with a weary smile. 'I really don't want to analyse my love life any more tonight.'

She just wanted to go home and be on her own.

She walked through to the staffroom, changed her clothes and made her way down the stairs to the car park. The battered old bicycle that she'd found in the garage of her rented cottage was exactly where she'd left it.

By the time she'd cycled home she was exhausted, but the minute she saw the red Italian sports car parked outside the cottage her exhaustion vanished.

No!

Surely he couldn't be…

Opening the front door slowly, Tia walked through to the kitchen and pushed open the door, stopping dead as she saw the man lounging there, one powerful thigh resting on the kitchen table, his cool, dark eyes steady on her shocked face.

'Luca…' One hand reached out blindly for the wall as she sought support.

She really, truly hadn't expected to see him again. Certainly not now. It had been two weeks.

Two weeks, and somehow she'd managed to diminish him in her mind. She'd blanked out just how much his physical presence affected her, forgotten how his blatant masculinity and unshakable self-confidence made her weak at the knees.

'Tia.' Thick, dark lashes swept down over his eyes, concealing his expression. He looked remote and unapproachable and she was suddenly totally unable to speak. Luca always did that to her. He was the only man in the world who rendered her completely tongue-tied.

She said the first thing that came into her head. 'How did you know where to find me?'

'I called Sharon.' His eyes lingered on her pale face. 'She gave me your address.'

Sharon?

'No.' Tia shook her head in disbelief but Luca's expression didn't change.

'Don't blame her. I didn't give her much choice. Let's just say I was…' he paused and searched for the right word '…persuasive.'

And Tia knew only too well just how persuasive Luca Zattoni could be when he wanted to be.

That explained why Sharon had looked so uncomfortable and guilty.

She glanced back towards the front door, still feeling shell-shocked by his unexpected presence. 'But presumably Sharon didn't provide you with a key?'

Luca lifted one broad shoulder dismissively. 'The sign was still outside and the letting agent was very helpful once I told him who I was. He seemed concerned about you living on your own here. This cottage is extremely isolated and you obviously aroused his protective instincts.'

It took a few moments for his words to sink in.

'The letting agent gave you a key?' She looked at him incredulously. 'Is there anyone you can't charm, Luca?'

'Apparently.' A ghost of a smile touched his firm mouth. 'Or presumably you wouldn't have left me standing at the altar two weeks ago,' he drawled, resting one lean brown hand on his muscular thigh. 'We have a great deal to talk about, *cara mia*.'

Her heart rate suddenly increased dramatically. 'We have nothing to talk about, Luca.'

Certainly not now, after a long day at the hospital. Tia hadn't been expecting this conversation and she had no idea how she was going to handle it. Was she going to confront him with what she'd discovered? Or was she going to wait for him to tell her the truth about his past, which he should have done right from the start? She needed to be prepared before she spoke to him. She needed to feel strong and in control.

As it was, all she felt was…vulnerable.

'Nothing to talk about?' He straightened in a fluid movement and strolled across the kitchen towards her. 'First you take flight on our wedding day without the slightest explanation, and next you leave the country, go back to your old job and rent a cottage in the middle of nowhere. We could talk for a week and not cover even half of what we have to discuss.'

Tia's throat was uncomfortably dry. 'I left you a note.'

'Ah, yes…' Thick lashes lowered slightly to shield his stunning dark eyes. 'The note that Sharon delivered, saying that you had changed your mind about marrying me.'

Her heart gave a little flip. She hadn't expected him to follow her and she wasn't prepared for this confrontation.

'It wouldn't have worked, Luca.' Her knees trembled slightly but she forced herself to hold his gaze. 'We were getting married for the wrong reasons. We—we didn't know each other properly.'

She hadn't known that he was involved in a serious, long-term relationship with another woman.

There was a long silence while he studied her face, the expression in his dark eyes unreadable. 'So, just like that, you leave?' His tone was even. 'You decide this by yourself, with no consultation with me? No attempt to discuss whatever problem you think exists? *Dio,* is that normal behaviour for two people who were planning to marry?'

Tia's breathing quickened and anger gripped her. *He* was criticising *her*? This was the time to confront him about what she'd heard, but she wasn't ready to do that yet. She didn't want to say something she'd regret. She needed time to think through the best way of tackling the subject.

Anyway, it was his responsibility to tell her about his past, to open up and tell her the truth.

'When would we have had this discussion, Luca?' She took refuge in attack. 'You were always at the hospital.'

His black brows met in a frown. 'Is that what this is all about? My working hours? I'm an obstetrician, Tia. You should understand the demands of the job better than most women.'

Suddenly she didn't feel at all well. She'd woken early that morning, been sick repeatedly and now he was expecting her to dissect their relationship. It was too much.

Her eyes closed briefly and she took a deep breath. 'Do we have to talk about this now?'

'Yes.' His voice was a deep growl and she flinched slightly. She'd always thought that Luca was very controlled, but suddenly he seemed like a stranger.

Which was part of the problem.

They didn't really know each other. That fact had been brought home to her with shocking clarity on the day of her wedding. She should never have agreed to marry him, but she'd been so swept away by the way he'd made her feel...

'We can meet up tomorrow or something,' she suggested, hoping that she wasn't going to embarrass herself by being sick in front of him. 'Where are you staying tonight?'

'Staying?' One dark eyebrow lifted as if her question was wholly irrelevant. 'Here, of course.'

'No way, Luca.' She shook her head vigorously. 'This is my cottage.'

Luca straightened in a fluid movement and moved purposefully towards her. 'And you're expecting our child,

Tia.' He said the words with careful emphasis. 'Your place is with me.'

'With you?' Her heart started to gallop. With him? Surely he wasn't serious—not after everything that had happened. 'You're not seriously suggesting that we should still get married?'

'Hardly.' His tone was dry. 'You've made your feelings on that subject very clear.'

Tia blushed slightly and looked away. Leaving him at the altar had been a lousy thing to do, but at the time she hadn't been able to see an alternative. She'd just needed to get away as fast as possible.

'So what exactly do you want, Luca?'

There was a slight pause. 'You,' he said softly. 'You and our baby.'

'Luca, no!' Her voice was suddenly hoarse and her heart was beating faster than she would have thought possible. 'It's time we were honest with each other. Our whole relationship was a mistake. We were just—very carried away…this baby wasn't planned.' Tia decided that it was time to voice at least some of her concerns. 'A month ago when I told you I was pregnant, you couldn't escape to the hospital fast enough!'

He tensed and his mouth tightened. 'That's not true.'

'It is true, Luca, and you know it.' Despite her best intentions, she felt her voice wobble slightly and forced herself to stay calm. The last thing she wanted was for him to know how badly his reaction had hurt her. She had too much pride. 'You were horrified to learn that I was pregnant and don't try and deny it because I'm excellent at reading body language and yours was shouting at me!'

His dark eyes were suddenly wary and for the first time since she'd met him he seemed slightly uncomfortable.

'You misunderstood me. It's true that the news of the baby came as a shock at first,' he admitted finally, his voice quiet. 'I would be less than honest if I didn't admit that I would have preferred us to have more time together before we considered having children, but—'

'You don't need to make excuses. I know that you weren't pleased, and nothing can change that.' Suddenly Tia felt hideously sick and she took several deep breaths to try and settle her stomach.

An ominous frown touched his forehead. 'Tia, when you first told me that you were pregnant, I hadn't been to bed for almost forty hours,' he said, his dark eyes intent on hers as he paused only inches away from her. 'I was called to one difficult delivery after another. By the time I saw you I was dead on my feet. The news that you were pregnant came as a shock, I admit that, and I probably didn't react the way I should have, but…'

Her eyes challenged him and she tried to ignore the effect that his closeness had on her. 'So you're saying that had you had a good night's sleep you would have been delighted?'

His dark gaze swept over her. 'You need to calm down, *cara mia*. You're very emotional.'

'Emotional?' Her jaw dropped and she gaped at him. 'Of course I'm emotional. We had three blissful weeks together in Venice, but when we moved back to your home in Milan you changed, Luca. I barely saw you. You spent every available minute at the hospital. When I finally found time to tell you that I was pregnant, you reacted as though it was the worst news I could have given you and vanished to the hospital again. Then you came home and proposed. But obviously for all the wrong reasons. I think I have every right to be emotional.'

Especially in view of what she'd found out since.

He muttered something under his breath in Italian and raked long fingers thought his glossy dark hair. 'Tia, I have already admitted that my reaction was less than perfect—'

'Understatement,' Tia muttered. 'Major understatement.'

A muscle worked in his jaw. 'I think we both need to calm down and then start this conversation again.'

'No.' She shook her head vigorously, desperate to get rid of him. Being so close to him eroded her will-power. 'There's nothing more to be said. This isn't about the baby, Luca, it's about us. You and I. And the fact that our hormones got tangled with our common sense.'

Nausea washed over her and she lifted a hand to her mouth. Oh, help! She was going to be sick again. She was sure of it.

Luca frowned sharply and his long, strong fingers curled into her shoulders. 'What's the matter? Are you ill?'

'No,' she lied, steadying her stomach with a few deep breaths. 'I'm just not enjoying this conversation. I want you to acknowledge that we both made a mistake so that we can move on.'

His hands dropped from her shoulders and his face might have been carved from stone. 'We're having a baby, Tia. It's too late to talk about making mistakes. We need to plan for the future.'

'Luca, we don't have a future,' she said firmly, genuinely amazed that he'd even suggest such a thing. But it was because of the baby, of course. Whatever his initial reaction had been, he'd clearly decided that responsibility should come before personal happiness. 'If a relationship isn't right without a baby then it certainly won't be right *with* a baby. We're totally wrong for each other. Discovering that I'm pregnant doesn't change that. I understand that you're upset because I left you at the altar, but—'

'I don't care about that,' Luca said dismissively. 'That is in the past, but the baby is in the future and our future is together.'

Tia stared at him. Sharon was obviously right. Luca Zattoni was a traditional Italian male to the core.

He might have been shocked originally, but the concept of family and children was so important to Italians that she should have guessed that, once he'd had time to think about it, there was no way that Luca would just dismiss the fact that she was pregnant.

'I am not going back to Italy with you, Luca.'

'You still haven't told me why you left Italy in the first place,' he said through gritted teeth. 'I can't believe that you changed your mind at the last minute. If you had doubts, why didn't you discuss them with me? *Dio*, I went up to your room and found everything gone. How did you think I felt?'

Remembering just what had made her leave in such a hurry, she looked at him without sympathy. 'I expect it damaged your ego.'

He muttered under his breath and gave her an impatient glance. 'Tia, I left the need to protect my ego behind in childhood, but I would be less than human if the unexplained disappearance of my bride-to-be—*my pregnant bride to be*—didn't disconcert me somewhat.'

'I thought you'd be pleased that I'd gone,' she mumbled, rubbing her toe on the kitchen floor and refusing to look at him. Having him so close was unsettling to say the least. She couldn't look at the man without remembering how they'd been together...

'I wasn't pleased,' he said softly, his Italian accent suddenly very pronounced as he accentuated every syllable.

She lifted her chin, her expression defiant. 'If you missed me so badly, if you were really that worried, why didn't you follow me straight away?'

He tensed and hesitated for only the briefest moment. 'There were complications,' he muttered finally. 'Things I needed to sort out.'

Luisa.

Tia turned away, hiding her hurt, but knowing that she'd done the right thing not to marry him. She didn't want to be anyone's second choice.

'You haven't told me why you changed your mind.'

'I—I had second thoughts,' she said honestly, flicking her hair back and looking him straight in the eye. 'I suddenly realised that there were so many things I didn't know about you.'

Luca frowned. 'Like what?'

Flustered, Tia avoided his question. 'I don't know, but it was all so fast and I don't think you should get married without knowing everything there is to know about the person you're marrying—'

'Tia there are always things about another person that stays hidden,' he said, and she shook her head.

'Not when you've known each other for a long time. When people have known each other for a long time they're as familiar as old socks.'

He lifted an eyebrow and looked at her incredulously. '*Dio.* That is your idea of a stimulating relationship? To live with someone who is like a sock?'

'I'm just trying to say—'

'It's all right—I think know what you're trying to say.' He let out a long breath and shook his head slowly. 'Tia, the length of a relationship is not always an indication of its depth.'

His voice was suddenly quiet and her heart suddenly missed a beat.

Was he going to tell her about Luisa?

Luca's jaw clenched. 'It's true that our relationship moved quickly and was very intense—'

Intense?

That had to be the understatement of the year.

She'd been so totally overwhelmed by what had been happening between them that she hadn't bothered to think about the future.

'But we weren't suited, Luca.'

'No? If my memory serves me correctly, we were never able to look at each other without needing to rip each other's clothes off,' he drawled softly. 'I wouldn't exactly describe that as ''not suited'', would you? You were in my bed the same night we met.'

His blunt reminder of just how quickly they'd become intimate brought a flood of colour to her cheeks and Tia closed her eyes. He was right, of course. The physical chemistry between them had been frighteningly powerful. It had completely swamped her common sense, what little she'd had, and it had clearly taken his mind off his troubles with Luisa.

'There's more to a relationship than good sex, Luca,' she said quietly, dragging her eyes away from his penetrating gaze and trying to regain some semblance of control.

The mere brush of those long, strong fingers against her flesh made her tremble and she struggled to hide it from him.

Dear God, why couldn't she just tell him the truth? That she knew he'd met her when his other relationship had been in trouble. That she knew he was in love with another woman.

He was watching her closely. 'You think our relationship was just about sex?'

For her, no, but for him?

'We're different, Luca,' she said finally. 'I—I didn't realise how different until we lived together in Milan. Perhaps if I'd had a job...'

The temperature in the room dropped below zero.

'There was no reason for you to work.' His jaw tightened and his expression was grim. 'I gave you credit cards—you weren't short of money.'

That was true enough. The Zattoni family were obviously extremely wealthy. She'd never had access to so much money in her life. But she didn't really care about money.

'It isn't about money, Luca,' Tia declared emphatically, trying to make him understand something of what she'd felt when they were in Italy. 'When we met in Venice it was beautiful—romantic. But Milan...'

'Milan is not Venice,' he agreed quietly, his eyes fixed on her pale face. 'Milan is more of a business city than a tourist one. It's foggy in winter and muggy in the summer and the pollution is grim.'

'I felt suffocated there,' Tia admitted, 'but it wasn't really the place. It was *us*. You spent all your time at the hospital and I was lonely.'

'Lonely?' He frowned sharply. 'You had the support of my family. How could you have been lonely?'

Tia's eyes slid away from his. 'They hate me, Luca,' she told him. 'They think I'm the wrong sort of woman for you, and do you know what?' She forced herself to meet that unsettling dark gaze head on. 'They're right. I *am* the wrong sort of woman. You should have married someone sleek and elegant, someone who'd know how to spend your money…'

It was the nearest she'd got to telling him that she knew about Luisa but not by the flicker of an eyelid did he betray himself.

'My family do not hate you.' His expression was suddenly ominous. 'What possible grounds do you have for making such a statement?'

She caught the look of disbelief in his eyes and decided to tell the truth.

'Luca, I never saw them,' she told him quietly, 'apart from the weekends when you and I visited them together.'

He muttered something under his breath in Italian. 'You spent most weekdays with them. Shopping, lunching.'

Tia gave a wry smile. 'No, Luca. Check your credit-card bill. I never once shopped or lunched. They never invited me and, anyway, I wouldn't have wanted to. I don't like spending money that way. That isn't the sort of life I'm used to and they knew that, which is presumably why they never invited me.'

Anger flashed in his black eyes and Tia winced. 'They're very traditional,' she said quickly, wishing she'd never said anything. She certainly didn't want to turn him against his family. 'They knew I wouldn't have been comfortable spending days with them.'

Luca's jaw was tight. 'So how did you spend your days?'

Tia gave a sad smile. They'd been together for three months and only now was he asking that question.

'I stayed in the flat and read books,' she told him, 'or I went for walks.'

He was suddenly tense. 'Milan is not a great city for walking. Where did you walk?'

She shrugged. 'Wherever took my fancy.'

'And you wouldn't have had the first clue where was safe and where wasn't.' He closed his eyes briefly. 'That evening we met in Venice, you were pacing the streets at night on your own. Do you have a death wish?'

'No, but I like to live my own life, and—'

'Tia, you are a stunningly beautiful woman,' he ground out angrily, 'and your blonde head shines like a beacon. It is very unusual to see a woman of your colouring in Italy and you attract no little amount of attention. You were putting yourself at risk.'

Without any warning her heart turned over. He thought she was beautiful?

No, that just didn't make sense. She was as unlike Luisa as it was possible to be.

Before she had a chance to digest this piece of information, his hands closed over her shoulders like a vice. 'I will talk to my family about their behaviour and you will promise me that you won't walk around on your own at night again.'

'I can't promise and I don't want you to talk to your family. There's no reason to. It's in the past now.' Suddenly Tia felt exhausted. Too exhausted to talk any further. 'It was all my fault, anyway. I am so far removed from a perfect Italian wife it's laughable. Your family did what they thought was best and they were right. I'm the sort of person who needs space and independence. I'm not the sort of person who enjoys shopping, lunching and beauty salons.'

She swayed slightly and Luca's grip on her shoulders tightened.

'We shouldn't be talking about this now.' He scooped her up as if she weighed nothing, holding her firmly against his chest. 'You're not well. You look pale and worn out. You need to go to bed.'

Bed.

Just thinking about bed when she was held this close to him made her body start to tremble. She could feel the hard muscle of his chest through the fabric of his shirt and her fingers itched to touch him.

No.

'Put me down, Luca.' She wriggled in his arms and then groaned and buried her head in his shoulder as everything swam.

He ignored her efforts to escape, his expression grim as he negotiated the narrow staircase that led upstairs.

'Where's your bedroom?'

'It's none of your business,' she protested weakly, wishing that being in his arms didn't feel quite so good. But she fancied him so much that her whole body melted if he so much as looked at her. It wasn't just that he was stunningly good-looking. There was something about him, an air of confidence and power, that was incredibly sexy.

Dear God, did she have no sense of self preservation?

How could she still feel this way about someone who didn't want her? How could her body still respond to him?

Luca shouldered open the few doors upstairs until he found what was obviously her bedroom and laid her gently on the bed.

'Our problem is that we are both too alike, you and I,' he told her, stroking the hair out of her eyes with gentle fingers and then checking her pulse. 'We are hot-tempered and stubborn. Why didn't you tell me that you felt ill? How long have you been in this state?'

Tia closed her eyes and fought back the waves of nausea. 'I'm not in a state. I'm just pregnant,' she mumbled, feeling drowsiness wash over her. She'd never felt so tired in her life. It was as if her body had turned off a switch and everything had shut down. She just had to sleep.

'Go away, Luca,' she murmured, fighting to stop her eyelids drooping. 'I want you to go home to Italy and leave me alone.'

She saw his eyes darken, knew she ought to finish the conversation but her body betrayed her, slowly drifting into sleep mode before she could resolve the situation. Her eyelids closed and she was dimly aware of Luca standing up and of having blankets tucked around her. Then darkness claimed her.

CHAPTER TWO

TIA awoke to the sound of rain thundering on the windows.

Remembering the evening before, she closed her eyes and gave a groan of mortification.

Luca.

She'd virtually passed out cold on the man. He'd carried her to her bed and…

Her eyes drifted to the clothes piled neatly on the chair in the corner of the room.

Her clothes.

Pushing back the duvet, she glanced down and saw that she was wearing one of Luca's old T-shirts. She ran her fingers over the soft fabric, her sensitive nose picking up his elusive male scent, the same scent that had wrapped itself around her on all those hot, steamy nights together.

The mere thought of his lean, brown hands touching her made her heart flip against her chest and a devastating weakness spread through her body.

Luca…

She'd never felt about anybody the way she felt about him.

And he must have undressed her last night.

Where had he stayed? Here? In the cottage? *Was he still here now?*

Tia sat up suddenly and swung her legs over the edge of the bed, anger bringing her to life.

How dared he?

How could Luca expect to stroll back into her life as if nothing had happened when he was in love with another woman? How dared he put her to bed and undress her? He was in no position to play happy families.

33

Her feet hit the floor and the sudden movement made her stomach churn.

She made it to the toilet just in time and retched miserably, wondering dully why any woman chose to get pregnant.

'You got up too quickly.' Luca's deep voice came from behind her and his long fingers lifted her hair away from her face.

'Go away, Luca.' She closed her eyes tightly, utterly humiliated that he should see her like this. Being ill was bad enough without having him witness it. 'I want some privacy.'

'I'm a doctor, *cara mia*,' he pointed out, his voice surprisingly gentle as he handed her a cool flannel. 'I see sick people every day.'

'I'm not people,' she said, wishing her stomach would settle. 'Leave me alone so I can die in peace.'

He murmured something in Italian and lifted her easily to her feet. 'You're not going to die. You have morning sickness. It should go by the fourteenth week.'

Tia slumped against the wall and looked at him with dull eyes. She was already twelve weeks pregnant. 'Another two weeks of this?'

He gave a faint smile, his dark eyes surprisingly sympathetic. 'Have you been sick much?'

'All the time,' Tia mumbled, and his smile faded as he switched into doctor mode.

'Do you have any pain when you are sick?'

'No.' She shook her head. 'Relax, Luca. I'm fine. Just pregnant.'

'You've lost weight.' His dark gaze raked over her slender frame and she looked at him, exhausted.

'Of course I've lost weight. The last few weeks haven't exactly been a picnic for me either, you know.'

'What has the doctor said about you?'

'What doctor?'

He frowned sharply. 'You haven't seen a doctor yet?'

She sighed. 'It's hardly been on the top of my list of priorities, Luca.'

'You should have had blood tests and a scan.' His eyes narrowed. 'When did you start your last period?'

'For goodness' sake!' She coloured, embarrassed by his question, and he muttered something under his breath and cupped her face in his hands.

'Tia, you are having my baby and I am a doctor,' he reminded her gently. 'You have no need to feel awkward. I need to ask you these things because I need to know that you are OK. Indulge me and answer the question. Please?'

'Twenty-fourth of July,' she muttered, feeling her cheeks heat again. They might have made the baby together but there was something about him that made her feel impossibly shy. 'Or, at least, that's what I think. I had some spotting a month later but not a real period. I worked out that I must be due on the 30th April.'

He nodded slowly. 'We need to get you booked in at the hospital and I want to send a urine specimen to check that you have no infection. It could be a reason for the vomiting.'

'Luca, I have morning sickness,' she said gruffly, strangely touched by his concern despite her mixed feelings towards him. 'It isn't hyperemesis.'

Hyperemesis gravidarum was a rare condition of pregnancy where nausea and vomiting were severe and could cause serious problems for the mother.

His expression was serious. 'Just how often have you been sick?'

'Quite a bit,' Tia confessed as she reached for her toothbrush. 'Usually whenever I'm tired. I suspect that you had a narrow escape last night. It's probably just as well you put me to bed early.'

He didn't laugh. 'Then you have to make sure that you don't get tired. It's your body telling you something.'

She brushed her teeth on autopilot and slowly sipped some water. 'Stop giving me orders, Luca.'

She put her toothbrush back in the cupboard and leaned her burning forehead against the cool glass of the bathroom cabinet. She felt terrible. She had to be at work in an hour and at the moment she could barely drag her body out of the bathroom. How did people get through nine months of this?

He held open the bathroom door and stood to one side. 'Go back to bed and I'll make you some breakfast.'

'Breakfast?' She shot him an incredulous look and put a protective hand on her abdomen. 'Are you some sort of sadist? Do you really think I'm hungry?'

'Food will help,' he reminded her gently, a glimmer of a smile touching his hard mouth. 'You're a midwife, Tia. You should know that eating something before you move in the morning can sometimes alleviate morning sickness. I'll fetch you some crackers.'

'There aren't any crackers,' she muttered, sliding past him, careful not to catch his eye. 'And stop ordering me around. You're not responsible for me. And while we're at it, you've got a nerve, undressing me while I'm asleep. And you had no right to stay the night.'

'You fell asleep in all your clothes,' he pointed out dryly. 'Hardly the most effective way of guaranteeing a good night's rest. And your prudishness is rather misplaced in the circumstances.'

Hot colour flooded Tia's cheeks. She knew what he was implying. That he knew her body better than she did. And it was all too true. The things that he could make her feel were scary.

'That was the past.' She said it to herself as much as him and started to walk down the stairs, holding tight to the bannisters to help support her wobbly knees. 'You no longer have the right to undress me.'

'I refuse to discuss this with you now.' His tone was

even as he followed her into the kitchen. 'Sit down and I'll make you some breakfast.'

She gaped at him, sure that she'd misheard.

Luca was offering to make her breakfast?

Well, that really was a first!

As far as she could recall, Luca couldn't so much as boil a kettle. He certainly hadn't done so in the three months that she'd known him.

'I thought Italian men were totally undomesticated,' she commented, watching with fascination as he yanked open cupboard after cupboard and finally tried the fridge. This was not a man who knew his way around a kitchen.

'*Dio*, there is nothing here! What were you planning to eat?' His tone was incredulous as he stared into the empty fridge. 'Thin air?'

'At least that won't upset my stomach,' she joked weakly, shrinking slightly at the black expression on his face. 'OK, there's no need to scowl. I haven't had time to shop yet. I was going to do it on my way home from work this evening.'

The minute she said it she could have bitten her tongue off. Bother. She hadn't intended to tell him about the job yet.

There was an ominous silence and Luca straightened up from his exploration of the empty fridge, his smooth dark brows locked in a frown.

'Work?' His eyes were suddenly cool. 'What do you mean, you were going to shop on the way home from work?'

She gave a long sigh. 'Luca, I'm going to be a single mother. I need a job—'

The fridge door closed with a muted thud. 'You are not going to be a single mother.'

'Luca...'

He walked towards her, his eyes flaming with anger and his broad shoulders tense. 'And you do not need a job.'

'I need to support myself, Luca.'

'You do not need to support yourself,' he said with icy cold clarity. 'That is my responsibility.'

She took a deep breath. 'But, you see, I don't want to be your responsibility. I need to work.'

'No,' he contradicted her fiercely. 'You do not need to work.'

Tia looked at him sadly. 'Which just goes to prove my point that we don't really know each other. If you knew me, you'd understand. But the truth is that our relationship is nothing more than a wild affair that got out of hand. And now we need to move on. I've been offered my old job back, Luca, and I intend to take it. In fact, I've already taken it. I've been working at the Infirmary for the past ten days. I'm surprised Sharon didn't mention it when you had your little chat.'

'Well, she didn't.' Luca stared at her, a muscle working in his dark jaw. 'Now that I am here to support you, give me one good reason why you need to work.'

His arrogance made her defiant. 'I don't have to give you a reason for anything I do. You can't bully me, Luca.'

A flush touched his tanned cheekbones and he had the grace to look uncomfortable. 'It was not my intention to bully you, merely to try and understand—'

'It's too late for that now,' she said stiffly, and his mouth tightened.

'It is not too late,' he ground out. 'We are having a baby and we stay together. And you will not work while you're pregnant.'

Tia stared at him, fascinated that he seemed so totally unashamed of blatantly expressing such chauvinistic opinions. Hadn't the man ever heard of equality or political correctness?

'Plenty of women work when they're pregnant.'

'But not you,' he growled, raking long fingers through his hair, clearly hanging onto control by a thread. 'I refuse to allow you to risk your health and our baby's health when you don't need to.'

Tia had always known that Luca was very traditional, but his flat dismissal of her new job was starting to make her blood boil.

'Stop trying to run my life,' she said angrily, wrapping her arms around her body in a gesture of self-protection. 'I have to work, Luca. For all sorts of reasons that you wouldn't begin to understand. Except for the few months I spent in Italy with you, I've always worked and fended for myself ever since I was young. I don't need or want to be supported. Especially now I'm back in England.'

Glittering dark eyes rested on her pink cheeks. 'But now you're pregnant,' he pointed out, his voice lethally soft, 'and I assume the reason that you were ill last night was because you were working all day. Am I right?'

Tia flinched at his tone but nodded slowly. 'Perhaps, but—'

'And then came home and virtually passed out,' Luca pointed out, sarcasm evident in his smooth tones as he cut through her attempts to justify herself. 'Working is obviously going to do you and the baby a world of good.'

'I just don't understand you.' Tia stared at him, baffled by the strength of his reaction. 'All of a sudden you're thinking about nothing but the baby. But when I first told you, you barely reacted. What's changed, Luca? Is this baby really so special to you, or is it just that you're such a primitive, unreconstructed male that you can't bear other people to see the mother of your child working?'

'Other people's opinion is of no interest to me whatsoever,' he responded grimly. 'But to answer your question, yes, of course the baby is special to me. And if you'd given me time to get used to the idea and not run off like a child in a tantrum, you would know that already. We could have discussed it.' His gaze was distinctly cool. 'But talking about things isn't something you're very good at, is it? You prefer to run and hide.'

Because all her life she'd had no one to rely on but herself.

It was obvious now that the baby was the reason he'd followed her. Luca was Italian through and through, with all the family values of his ancestors. There was no way a man like him would let his pregnant wife leave. Even if he did regret marrying her.

She tried hard to pull herself together. She'd known that he didn't love her so why did it hurt so much that he wanted their marriage to work because of the baby?

'Like I said last night, the baby isn't the issue here,' she said stiffly. 'It's our relationship, Luca. We—we don't really know each other.'

His eyes locked with hers, his expression impossible to read. 'Then we will get to know each other.'

She looked at him with exasperation. 'Luca, this is ridiculous. We're completely wrong for each other.'

Not least because he was still in love with someone else. All right, he might be here with her at the moment but that was clearly because of the baby, not because he was in love with her. Had the man once mentioned the word 'love'? No.

'If we don't know each other,' he said smoothly, 'then how can you possibly know that we are wrong for each other?'

She bit her lip. 'I just do.'

'You're talking nonsense. One of the reasons we haven't talked much is because we spent the whole time making love,' he reminded her gently, and Tia's cheeks coloured at the look in his eyes.

It was absolutely true.

They'd been unable to spend time together without ending up in bed. Even when they'd returned from Venice and Luca had been working all hours, their physical relationship had sizzled with passion. Tired or not, where sex was concerned the man was one hundred per cent hot Italian.

There was a long silence and Luca's gaze roved slowly over her flushed cheeks and rested on her mouth. She knew that he was remembering those nights, too, and heat pooled in the pit of her stomach.

'There is a simple solution to all this,' he said softly, dragging his eyes back to hers. 'If you think we don't know each other, then we get to know each other.'

Tia shook her head. 'It's too late for that, Luca. You want someone to stay at home and keep house, someone who will happily spend your money and rely on you. I'm not like that. I've never relied on anyone in my life. I can't do it. I'm not the right woman for you.'

'You are having my baby,' he said steadily, his eyes never leaving hers. 'That makes you the right woman.'

Tia opened her mouth to argue and then noticed the clock on the wall and gave a gasp of horror. She was going to be late. Was that his plan? To make her so late they wouldn't want her working for them?

'I don't have time for this, Luca,' she muttered, standing up and making for the kitchen door. 'I'm going to have a shower and then I'm going to work. I don't know what time your flight back to Italy is but you can stay in the cottage until you go. Just post the keys through the door when you leave.'

Without waiting to hear his reply, she left the room, trying not to look at the grim set of his firm mouth.

It was obvious that Luca still had plenty to say on the subject but it was going to have to wait. She didn't intend to jeopardise her job for anyone.

She needed to work and she wanted to work, and no chauvinistic Italian was going to stop her. However much he made her knees knock.

*   *   *

Despite her worries about the time, Tia arrived early and the first person she saw was Sharon.

'Are you mad at me?'

Tia slung her bag into her locker and changed into her uniform. 'I should be.'

'But you're not?' Sharon looked at her hopefully. 'What happened? What did he say about Luisa?'

Tia turned the key in her locker. 'I didn't mention Luisa.'

'Why?' Sharon looked horrified and Tia stopped dead and let out a long breath.

'Because I want him to tell me himself, not just because he thinks he's been found out.' Her chin lifted. 'I don't want a relationship where we have secrets. Remember my parents? When my mother found out about my father's affairs she was devastated. She'd always trusted him.' Tia felt the familiar feeling of anger swell inside her. Anger towards the man who'd ruined her mother's life. 'I will not have a relationship with someone who keeps secrets.'

Sharon's expression was cautious. 'But what did he say? Did he just want to yell at you for leaving him at the altar?'

Tia frowned. 'Funnily enough, that hardly figured in the conversation. I'll say this for the man, he's a very cool customer. He seemed almost indifferent to the chaos I caused. He was more concerned with discussing the future.'

Sharon's eyes widened. 'So there is a future?'

Tia shook her head. 'Not as far as I'm concerned. He obviously wants to be around for the baby, but that's not enough for me.'

Sharon looked puzzled. 'Are you sure that's really the reason?'

'Of course.' Tia pulled herself together, dropped the locker key in her pocket and made for the door. 'I need to get on. Mrs Adams was about to feed the baby when I walked past so I said I'd help her. I'll do her check afterwards.'

'OK, thanks.' Sharon followed her out of the staffroom and Tia made her way to the four-bedded side ward.

'Hello, Fiona. How's the feeding going?'

'Really well.' Fiona looked up with a smile. 'Someone's helped me put her on the breast every time, but she seems to latch on really well and she only fed three times in the night. I thought that was pretty good.'

'Absolutely.' Tia leaned over the cot and stroked the downy head with a gentle finger. 'Were you a good girl for Mummy? Did you agree on a name?'

Fiona nodded. 'She's going to be Megan.'

'Nice. Well, in that case, Megan, it's time for breakfast.' She scooped the baby up firmly and handed her to Fiona, watching carefully as Fiona tried to put the baby on the breast herself.

'That's great, Fiona. You've both really got the hang of it.'

Tia stayed with Fiona until she was happy that the baby was feeding nicely and then moved on to help another new mother.

Before she'd even pulled the curtains around the bed, Sharon called her.

'Sorry, Tia, would you mind going up to labour ward to give them a hand? They've had six admissions in the last two hours.' Sharon rolled her eyes and walked up the corridor with Tia. 'Chaos. And, of course, they'll all end up down here.'

So Tia hurried to the labour ward and introduced herself to Nina, the midwife in charge.

'Would you mind looking after Mrs Henson for the time being?' Nina checked her notebook. 'She's only four centimetres and not coping well at all. We've bleeped the anaesthetist and he's coming to do an epidural. And do you mind having one of the student midwives in with you? She needs to get a few more deliveries.'

Tia nodded. Student midwives had to deliver a certain

number of babies under supervision before they were allowed to qualify.

Dawn Henson was a twenty-two-year-old woman, having her first baby, and one look at her face was enough for Tia to realise that she was terrified.

'The pain is so much worse than I imagined,' she gasped, her knuckles white as she grasped her husband's hand. 'I really, really wanted to have a natural birth but I don't think I can stand it. I feel such a failure.'

'You're not a failure, Dawn,' Tia said firmly. 'Labour isn't a competition. The pain is different for each individual and everyone copes in different ways. I think you've made a wise decision to have an epidural.'

Dawn bit her lip. 'But I didn't really want to have one. I'm terrified of having a needle in my spine. What if it goes wrong?'

'It won't go wrong.' Tia looked up as Duncan Fraser, one of the anaesthetic consultants, walked into the room. 'Here's the person to talk to. Dr Fraser will explain everything to you.'

Signalling with her eyes that Dawn was more than a little anxious, Tia busied herself getting things ready for the anaesthetist.

Duncan talked quietly to the couple for a few minutes, explaining the procedure and the risks involved, pausing while Dawn had another contraction.

'OK, I need to start by putting a drip in your arm.'

Tia handed him a wide-bore cannula and Kim, the student midwife, checked Dawn's blood pressure.

'All right, Dawn, I want you to sit on the edge of the trolley for me—that's it.' Tia helped her to adjust her position until she was as comfortable as possible and waited while Duncan scrubbed up.

He put on a sterile gown and gloves and positioned himself behind Dawn. 'All right, I want you to tell me if you feel a contraction coming so that I can stop,' he said quietly as he gave the local anaesthetic into the skin.

Duncan nicked the skin with the scalpel and introduced the Tuohy needle, advancing it cautiously towards the epidural space. He checked that the needle was in the right place and Tia watched Dawn carefully, knowing that even the slightest movement at this stage could result in a dural puncture with unpleasant consequences for the patient.

Fortunately Dawn remained still and Duncan quickly threaded the epidural catheter through the needle and withdrew the needle.

'All right Dawn.' Duncan glanced up briefly and then returned to his task. 'I'm going to inject a small dose of anaesthetic now.'

He gave a test dose and then taped the epidural catheter in place and attached an antibacterial filter to the end. Tia timed five minutes and then checked the blood pressure.

Satisfied with the reading, Duncan gave the remainder of the anaesthetic dose.

'All right, Dawn, Tia is going to need to check your blood pressure every five minutes for the first twenty minutes just to check that it doesn't drop.'

Dawn gave him a grateful smile. 'I can feel it working already—the pain is nowhere near as bad.'

'Good.' Duncan gave her a warm smile, talked to Tia about giving top-ups and then left the room.

Now that the pain had gone, Dawn's face regained some of its colour and she was a great deal happier.

'Will I still be able to push the baby out?'

'We'll certainly aim for that,' Tia told her, checking her blood pressure again and recording it on the chart. 'As you progress towards the end of the first stage of your labour, we'll let the epidural wear off so that you can feel to push.'

It was towards the end of her shift when Dawn started pushing and the baby was delivered normally, with the minimum of fuss. Tia quietly praised Kim who had performed a textbook delivery.

'I can't believe it's all over.' Dawn collapsed, exhausted, her face pale. 'I can't believe we've got a little girl. We've only thought of boys' names, haven't we, Ken?'

Her husband gave a shaky laugh. 'We'd better start thinking fast.'

Tia gave an absent smile, her eyes on the student midwife. The placenta wasn't coming away as quickly as it should and Kim was obviously concerned. Tia knew that with the use of oxytocic drugs and controlled cord traction, the third stage of labour—the delivery of the placenta—was usually completed in ten minutes in the majority of labours.

In Dawn's case they were well past ten minutes and Tia was well aware that there was a danger of bleeding if the placenta was retained.

'Stop using cord traction,' she instructed Kim in a low voice. 'There's a risk that the cord might snap or the uterus might invert.'

Tia pressed the buzzer to call for help and then palpated Dawn's abdomen. If the uterus was well contracted then it could mean that the placenta had separated but was trapped by the cervix.

Outwardly calm, still making small talk about the baby, Tia gently palpated the uterus with her fingertips. Instead of feeling firm and contracted, it felt soft and distended and her heart gave a little lurch.

She massaged the top of the uterus with a smooth, circular motion, careful not to apply too much pressure.

'Is something wrong?' Dawn looked at her with tired eyes and Tia gave her a reassuring smile, noting that she seemed very pale and restless.

'Your placenta isn't separating as quickly as it should do,' she said carefully, 'so we'll just get the doctor to take a look at you. Nothing for you to worry about, Dawn.'

Sharon entered the room seconds later, her eyebrows lifted questioningly.

'I think we may have a retained placenta here. Can you bleep the senior reg?' Tia asked quickly, and Sharon nodded immediately.

'Will do.'

'Put the baby on the breast, Kim,' Tia instructed quietly, and the student immediately did as requested, understanding that the action of breast feeding could help the uterus contract. Tia tried to rub up a contraction and just as she was starting to feel seriously worried the doors slammed open and Sharon hurried in, closely followed by—

Luca.

Tia's heart kicked against her ribs and she turned incredulous eyes to Sharon who merely shrugged helplessly, indicating from her expression that she didn't know what was going on.

Luca barely gave her a second glance, instead striding straight to the bed and introducing himself to Dawn. Tia immediately snapped back into professional mode, her personal feelings towards him temporarily forgotten. Now wasn't the time to question his presence.

'It seems as though she has a retained placenta,' she told him quickly, 'She delivered forty minutes ago. The uterus is atonic. I've tried to rub up a contraction, we've put the baby to the breast.'

Luca started scrubbing, firing questions at her over his shoulder. 'Has she emptied her bladder?'

'We've just catheterised her,' Tia told him, 'and we've got everything ready to set up an IV.'

'She's had an epidural?'

Tia nodded. 'Yes, but it's wearing off.'

'Let's top it up immediately and bleep the anaesthetist. I want her transferred to Theatre,' Luca instructed, turning to his SHO who was hovering. 'Can you sort out the epidural top-up and the IV, please, Dr Ford? Take blood for haemoglobin and cross-matching.'

Despite the emergency, the glamorous, dark-haired SHO couldn't stop sneaking looks at Luca, and Tia found herself grinding her teeth as they moved Dawn into Theatre.

Luca walked quickly over to the head of the bed and gave the frightened woman a reassuring smile.

'Dawn, your placenta does not want to come away by itself so I'm going to have to help it out,' he said quietly, his Italian accent giving his words a warm and attractive quality. 'You still have the anaesthetic in place so it shouldn't be painful, but if I hurt you in any way I want you to tell me immediately. We will work as a team, I promise.'

Tia watched with awe as he calmed both Dawn and her husband with his quiet confidence and then prepared for a manual removal of the placenta.

Tia bit her lip. She'd actually never seen a placenta removed like this before. She'd read about it, of course, but she'd never actually seen it happen and she was heartily relieved that Luca was there to take charge. There were stories of exceptional circumstances when a doctor couldn't be found and a midwife had had to undertake the procedure. Frankly, the thought made her shudder.

Sharon hovered at the back of the room, knowing that she could have a serious emergency on her hands.

'She has a partial separation,' Luca told the SHO as he examined Dawn. 'The fundus is broad, whereas it should be contracted, and she is losing some blood.'

Actually, that was an understatement, Tia thought anxiously. Dawn was now bleeding steadily and she watched as Luca covered his hand in antiseptic cream and introduced it carefully into the vagina, following the line of the cord which he held tight with his other hand.

Then he released the cord and transferred his free hand to Dawn's abdomen.

'I can feel the separated edge…' Luca's handsome face was a mask of concentration as he worked his fingers between the placenta and the uterine wall.

Tia watched, fascinated despite her anxiety for Dawn, noting that he used his free hand to press on Dawn's abdomen to prevent tearing of the lower segment of the uterus.

With a grunt of satisfaction, Luca rubbed up a contraction and gently removed his hand, dropping the placenta into a kidney-dish. 'There. OK, we need to check that this is intact.'

Tia adjusted the light and they examined the placenta thoroughly to check that none of it had been retained within the uterus.

When he was satisfied that the placenta was complete Luca turned his attention back to the mother.

'Everything is fine, Dawn,' he said quietly, examining her abdomen again. 'Your uterus is well contracted now and the bleeding has stopped. We'll check your haemoglobin level but I don't think that the blood you have lost will cause you a problem.' He turned back to his SHO. 'Give her some more oxytocin and start antibiotics.'

'Yes, Dr Zattoni.' The SHO was gazing at Luca as if he was the answer to her prayers, and Tia was filled with a sudden insecurity.

It didn't matter whether Luca was in love with Luisa or not—he would always have women throwing themselves at him. And would he be able to resist them? She knew better than most that plenty of men wouldn't.

Men like her father.

Feeling sick at the thought she looked for an excuse to leave the room.

'I'll go and phone the ward,' she mumbled, desperate to get away from the sight of Luca talking to the glamorous SHO. In fact, she could have used the phone in Theatre but she needed some space to calm herself down.

Sharon was hot on her heels as she made for the desk. 'Look, I'm really sorry. Believe me, I had no idea—'

'It doesn't matter.' Tia sat down on the nearest chair and took several deep breaths.

Sharon looked at her anxiously. 'Prof told me he had a new senior reg, but I didn't bother asking the name and I didn't even know he was due to start today. When I rang Switchboard they just told me that a Dr Zattoni was on call—I had no opportunity to warn you.'

'It doesn't matter,' Tia repeated, feeling a rush of relief as her stomach calmed down.

Sharon looked totally confused. 'But he couldn't have arranged this overnight. Did he tell you last night that he'd applied for a job here?'

'No, of course not.' Tia's voice was gruff and her eyes were slightly too bright. 'He doesn't tell me anything, remember?'

Sharon shifted slightly and glanced back along the corridor. 'He's a damn good doctor, Tia—that was an incredible performance back there.'

Tia nodded, a slight frown touching her brows. She'd never seen Luca in action before and he'd certainly been impressive.

Hoping that Sharon would drop the subject, she picked up the phone and called the postnatal ward just to warn them that Dawn would be on her way shortly and to brief them on what had happened so that they could monitor her condition.

'Well, he's obviously not thinking of returning to Italy any time soon,' Sharon said quietly, and Tia looked at her.

'No.' She summoned up a smile for the sake of appearances, trying not to think about what it would do for her pulse rate to see Luca at such close quarters every day.

'Which means that he can't possibly be involved with Luisa.'

'Does it?' Tia closed her eyes and let out a sigh.

What a mess.

Sharon sat down on the chair next to her, her voice soft. 'He wants you, Tia.'

Tia gave a crooked smile. 'Or does he just want the baby. If it hadn't been for the baby, he'd have patched things up with Luisa, remember?'

Sharon sighed. 'Tia, you have to talk to him about it.'

'No.' Tia lifted her chin stubbornly. 'He has to be the one to talk to me.'

Picking up the phone to end the conversation, she called a porter to come and help with Dawn and finished completing her section of the notes.

Luca strolled up to the desk, his shoulders looking broader than ever under the white coat.

'Have you finished your shift?'

Tia stared at him defiantly, still furious that he hadn't told her that he'd be working in the same hospital as her.

'No.'

'Yes.' Sharon corrected her with a frown, glancing across at Kim. 'Kim, would you mind taking Dawn up to the ward? Tia's already spoken to them so they're expecting her.'

Tia stood up. 'I'll—'

'It's already past the end of your shift and you're exhausted,' Sharon said firmly, avoiding Tia's eyes. 'Go home.'

Tia almost growled out loud. She was more than ready to go home but she didn't want to go with Luca.

'All right.' She stood up. 'But I'll make my own way.'

Luca's jaw tightened but he said nothing in front of her colleagues, instead choosing to follow her into the staff-room.

'Luca, this is the female changing room,' she pointed out, trying not to notice just how good he looked with his powerful body planted firmly in front of the door.

He shrugged dismissively. 'I have something to say to you and I assumed you didn't want me to say it in public.'

She yanked open the door of the locker, unable to keep the sarcasm out of her tone. 'I'm amazed you want to talk to me at all. What's the point of having a conversation when one misses out important details like, ''By the way, Tia, I'll be starting a new job in your hospital tomorrow.'''

And that was just for starters. She knew only too well what other important fact he was keeping from her.

'I didn't mention it because I didn't know that I would be starting today,' Luca said evenly. 'In fact, I didn't know that I would be starting at all. I have had several conversations with the hospital but it was only confirmed this morning. It seems that they are in a crisis. Someone is off with food poisoning and someone else has taken compassionate leave. So, instead of starting in a week's time, I agreed to start immediately.'

'But you could at least have mentioned it,' Tia pointed out, her eyes blazing as she dragged her clothes out of her locker.

Luca frowned. 'Nothing was confirmed and we had other, more important matters to discuss, as I recall.'

Tia stared at him in exasperation. 'But you didn't even tell me that you were applying for a job in England, and yet you must have applied months ago.'

There was a long silence and a strange look flickered across Luca's handsome face.

'Just after we met,' he admitted finally, and Tia let out a disbelieving breath.

'And it didn't seem relevant to mention that either? Well, believe it or not, I like to know what's going on,' Tia said, stripping off her cotton bottoms and dragging on her jeans. She took hold of the hem of her top and then hesitated. 'Look the other way.'

Their eyes clashed and a sharp stab of electricity shot through her body and weakened her knees.

He clearly thought it was crazy to look the other way when he'd seen her naked more times than he could count.

'We don't have that sort of relationship any more, Luca,' she croaked, tightening her fingers on her tunic.

Muttering something under his breath, he turned his back, the tension visible in his broad shoulders.

She changed quickly and pushed her clothes into her bag. 'You can look now.'

'Thank you.' His ironic glance was at odds with his courteous tone and she looked at him warily.

'Now what?'

'Now we go home and finish the conversation we were having when you passed out on me last night,' he said softly. 'My car is in the car park.'

She slung her bag over her shoulder. 'Thanks, but I'll make my own way home.'

His mouth tightened into a grim line. 'On that contraption you call a bike? No way. You have been working all day and you are exhausted, Tia. I will give you a lift.'

She glared at him and then smiled sweetly. 'Will my bike fit in the boot of your car?'

Luca winced visibly at the thought. 'You can leave it here.'

'Overnight?' She shook her head. 'No way. Someone might steal it.'

'Steal it?' His incredulous tone and the lift of his dark eyebrows told her clearly what he thought of that suggestion. 'Tia, it is a heap of rusty metal. No one in their right mind would steal it.'

She opened her mouth to argue again and then closed it again. The truth was she *was* totally exhausted. She'd never felt so tired in her life and the thought of cycling the five miles home was almost laughable.

'All right.' She knew she sounded ungracious but she couldn't help it. 'We'll go in your car.'

'Good.' For a moment she thought she saw humour

gleam in his dark eyes but then it was gone and he held
the door open for her. 'Let's go.'

They walked in silence out of the building. Just as they
were crossing the car park, the glamorous Dr Ford dashed
up to Luca, wanting him to check some trivial detail on a
drug chart.

All Tia's fears flooded back. Was Luca interested in the
woman? She was certainly attractive and she was totally
ignoring Tia.

On impulse she slipped an arm through his. 'Hurry up,
darling,' she whispered in her sexiest voice. 'I've been
waiting to go home with you all day.'

Luca went still and she saw surprise flicker briefly in his
eyes. And she could hardly blame him for that! She was
pretty shocked herself. Whatever had possessed her? One
minute she was keeping him at arm's length and the next
she was ready to claw Dr Ford's eyes out...

Embarrassed and confused by her own behaviour, Tia
gingerly released his arm and shrank quietly into the background as Luca turned back to the SHO, scribbled something on the chart and issued some brief instructions.

As Dr Ford walked back across the car park, Luca turned
to her, his gaze uncomfortably penetrating.

'Well?'

'Well, what?' Still feeling embarrassed, Tia yanked the
car door open so hard that she nearly removed it from its
hinges.

One eyebrow swooped upwards. 'I need to spell it out?'

Tia glared at him. 'She was drooling all over you, Luca.'

He turned his head to watch the retreating woman and
then looked back at her, his eyes narrowing. 'Dr Ford?
You're imagining things.'

'Oh, come on.' Had he really not noticed? 'She's crazy
about you and she's only just met you and she's probably
the first of many. I suppose the whole hospital will be
drooling over you by the end of the week.'

'Drooling?' The expression in his dark eyes was stunned. 'I'm a doctor, Tia, not some sort of sex symbol.'

Tia bit her lip. How had Sharon described him? *Sex on legs.*

Did he really have no idea how attractive he was to women?

'Think about it, Luca,' she mumbled. 'Was that really an important question she asked you or was she finding reasons to speak to you?'

He opened his mouth and closed it again, staring at her thoughtfully. 'She's my SHO, Tia.'

'You don't need to tell me that.' Tia gritted her teeth. 'She's been ogling you all afternoon.'

'Ogling?' His face was blank and suddenly he sounded very Italian. 'What is ogling?'

Tia tipped her head back. 'Staring at you, making eyes at you, flirting.'

'You're imagining things.' His tone was calm but his gaze was speculative as it rested on her face. 'She is my SHO. We have to speak to each other. We certainly weren't flirting.'

Had he really not noticed? 'She couldn't take her eyes off you, Luca.'

'And you were jealous.' His quiet statement was more than a little smug and her chin lifted.

'Jealous?' She gave a short laugh that sounded false even to her ears. 'Are all Italians as arrogant and self-confident as you? I wasn't jealous, Luca.'

Being jealous would mean that she wanted him—and she didn't, did she?

'You have no reason to be jealous,' he told her, carefully ignoring her comment about Italians.

She slid into the car and waited for him to start the engine.

'When you are angry, your eyes turn a very interesting shade of green,' Luca observed mildly, pulling out of the car park and onto the main road. 'I noticed it the first night we met when I made the mistake of trying to tell you that you shouldn't be hanging around a bus station at night.'

'I shouted at you, didn't I?' Tia shot him a sideways look that bordered on the apologetic. 'I'm not very good at being told what to do,' she confessed grudgingly, and he gave a laugh of genuine amusement.

'So I am beginning to learn.' An unbearably sexy smile tugged at the corner of his mouth as he glanced towards her. 'It certainly makes for an interesting and unpredictable relationship, *cara mia.*'

But did they have a relationship?

Tia got ready to argue but found she didn't have the energy. She shouldn't have agreed to help out by working the extra hours.

Maybe if she closed her eyes for just a few minutes she'd have enough energy to deal with Luca once they arrived home.

She had a feeling she was going to need it.

CHAPTER THREE

WHEN Tia opened her eyes again she was lying on the sofa with a blanket tucked around her.

'So you're finally awake.' Luca placed a mug of tea on the low table next to her and sat down on the end of the sofa. 'I must admit you're scintillating company when you're pregnant.'

She struggled to sit up, feeling decidedly groggy and disorientated. She had no recollection of how she'd got into the house. 'Did I sleep in the car?'

'Like a dead person,' Luca said dryly, his eyes scanning her quickly. 'Collapsing on me seems to be becoming a habit. It's a good job you don't weigh very much.'

Which was nonsense, she knew. Luca was incredibly strong and athletic—more than capable of lifting someone twice her weight.

'I'm sorry,' she mumbled, wishing that he wasn't sitting quite so close to her. She could see the taut muscle of his thigh under the material of his trousers and her throat closed.

She wanted him so badly it was almost a physical ache.

How could she still want a man who was in love with another woman? How could she still want a man who had kept such an enormous secret from her? How could she be in love with someone whose view of women seemed to be firmly set in the Stone Age?

Their eyes met and held and she felt her heart rate increase alarmingly. Then Luca stood up suddenly, his voice rough.

'I've made you something to eat.' He strode back into the kitchen and returned carrying a tray.

Tia stared in disbelief at the strange mass on the plate. 'Wh-what is it?'

He followed her gaze and shifted slightly. 'It's an omelette,' he said stiffly. 'I couldn't find a recipe book.'

A recipe book? For an omelette?

Staggered that he'd tried to cook something for her, Tia hid a smile, knowing that his male pride was at stake. After all, it wasn't entirely his fault that he was so undomesticated. From what she'd seen, it was his upbringing.

Whenever they'd stayed with Luca's family she had been appalled by the way they waited on him. No matter that Luca's sisters were both intelligent, they seemed not to question their role in nurturing their brother and Tia had spent more time holding a teatowel than a conversation.

But here he was, cooking for her. Or at least trying to!

She picked up a fork and started to eat.

'Does it taste all right?' His need for reassurance was so unlike Luca that she almost dropped the fork.

Was this really the same arrogant, self-assured man she'd known in Italy? It was the first time she'd ever witnessed him express doubt about anything. Was he really seeking her approval for something as simple as an omelette?

'It tastes great,' she said finally, unable to resist teasing him slightly. 'Better than it looks.'

After a moment's hesitation he returned the smile, his cheeks creasing in the way that made her heart stop. Luca Zattoni was without doubt the sexiest man she'd ever seen, and no matter what he did she would probably always want him.

The thought effectively removed her appetite and she put the fork down on the plate with a clatter and a shake of her head.

'I'm sorry, Luca, but I'm not really hungry,' she said quietly, her eyes sliding away from his. 'It isn't your omelette—really. It's…nice and I'm grateful to you but…'

He watched her steadily and for a wild, uncomfortable

moment she thought he must have guessed the reason for her sudden lack of appetite. But he merely removed the plate without comment, shifting slightly on the sofa so that he was facing her.

'In that case, this is as good a time as any to finish our talk. You've had a sleep, so hopefully we should manage it without you being sick or passing out.'

There was still a trace of humour in his voice but this time Tia didn't respond. Suddenly she did feel sick—but with misery.

What was she going to do? She'd thought that it would be easy to get over him. That he wouldn't affect her any more. But it just wasn't the case. One look—one smile— and she had serious trouble with her breathing.

She bit her lip, angry with herself. How had she ever let one man affect her as much as Luca? And so quickly. It was just a physical thing. It must be.

'I don't know what there is to talk about, Luca,' she said, concentrating on her tea and on not looking at him. If she didn't look at him it should theoretically be possible to keep her pulse rate within the normal range. 'I'm not going to marry you.'

'I'm not asking you to.'

Savage disappointment twisted her insides and she felt a lump building in her throat.

'Right.' She looked up at him and gave him a wobbly smile. 'So you agree that our relationship is over...'

He frowned. 'I agree to nothing of the sort,' he said, stretching out a hand and smoothing a stray strand of blonde hair out of her eyes. 'I merely said that I'm not asking you to marry me. Our relationship is very much alive.'

Her heart thudded against her rib cage. 'We were wrong to get involved so quickly, Luca.'

When he was still involved with someone else.

He sighed and something like regret flickered across his face. 'It's true that we could have taken things slower...'

It was the nearest he'd ever come to admitting to her that their relationship had been a mistake.

'Right,' she said shakily, trying to ignore the feeling of sick disappointment that he hadn't contradicted her. 'Well, there's nothing more to be said, is there?'

'On the contrary, there's plenty I need to say.' He stood up abruptly and paced across the room to the window, his shoulders tense as he stared into the darkness.

He paused and then turned to face Tia, his expression serious. 'I have thought carefully about what you said last night and I can see now that being in Italy wasn't easy for you. I was working much of the time and I accept now that my family may not have been as supportive as they should have been. I intend to speak to them about that.'

Tia's eyes widened. He was admitting that fault might have been on his side? For a man as autocratic and proud as Luca, that was quite an admission.

'Luca—'

'Let me finish.' He turned to face her, a light frown touching his dark brows. 'I'm sorry that you feel that I was never around, but there were certain factors which meant that I was at the hospital more than I would have liked.'

What factors? Luisa?

'And what about the baby? How do you really feel about the baby?' Her voice was little more than a croak and a smile pulled at his firm mouth.

'We both know that we made that baby the first night we met, *cara mia*.' His voice was suddenly soft. 'And I blame myself for that entirely. I should have had more control.'

Tia coloured. 'I was there, too. And I still can't believe I slept with you on the first night. I'd never—' She broke off and looked away, cursing herself for being so honest. *She'd never meant to tell him.*

'You'd never slept with a man before,' he finished gently. 'Did you really think I didn't know that? I knew almost from the first moment I met you. You were very inexperienced and naïve. It was one of the reasons I was worried about you wandering the streets at night. You are very independent and feisty but also very innocent, and it shows.'

'Oh.' Tia stared at him stupidly. 'I didn't want to tell you.'

He'd been so sophisticated and self-confident, so unlike the men—*boys*—she usually met.

'You are a stunningly beautiful girl, Tia, and there is an incredible attraction between us, otherwise perhaps I would have had the strength of will to take things more slowly. That night was unbelievably erotic,' he murmured softly, his eyes wandering slowly over her flushed cheeks, 'which is, of course, why we find ourselves in this position now.'

Her eyes moved warily to his and then slid away again. It was impossible not to be affected by Luca's looks, she thought helplessly. It wasn't just his eyes that reflected the raw nature of his masculinity, it was everything about him. The hard lines of his cheekbones, the dark shadow of his jawline.

She gave a small sigh, acknowledging the fact that no woman in her right mind would turn down the advances of a man like Luca. It was hardly surprising she'd lost all her morals and common sense. One look from those dark eyes and she'd been lost.

'We— I suppose we both got carried away,' she responded, and he gave a half-smile.

'I think that's probably a rather limp description of what happens between you and I, *cara mia*.' His eyes dropped to her mouth and she felt her heart rate increase rapidly in response to his gaze. 'I have a suggestion about our relationship.'

She licked dry lips. 'What?'

'You say that we got involved too quickly.' His eyes returned to hers and held them. 'That you don't really know me.'

'That's right.' Her voice was little more than a whisper. 'The physical side just overwhelmed everything.'

Including common sense.

His eyes darkened slightly and she knew he was remembering just how good it had been between them.

'You were very inexperienced so I can see how that might have been the case. So what I suggest,' he said roughly, 'is that we start again. Slow things down. Take time to get to know each other.'

She stared at him, her breathing rapid as she listened to him. He was seriously suggesting that they carry on their relationship?

What about Luisa?

'I—I don't know, Luca,' she said, raking her hair away from her forehead with shaking fingers. 'I need to think about it.'

'There's nothing to think about,' he said smoothly, walking back across the room and standing in front of her. As always, he was supremely confident and sure of himself. 'You yourself said that we don't know each other well enough, so let's put that right. Spending some time together will show us whether we can truly love each other or not. We owe it to our child to at least find that out.'

She winced at the cold brutality of his words. She already knew that he didn't love her, of course, but hearing him spell it out hurt more than she possibly could have imagined.

'Tia?' His firm tone made her glance up and she realised that he was waiting for her to say something.

And she didn't know what to say.

She loved Luca, she knew that, and she wanted to be with him, but not if he didn't want to be with her. Not if he only wanted their relationship to work because of the baby.

She lifted her chin. 'It wouldn't work.'

A muscle worked in his jaw and he took a deep breath. 'Think about it, Tia.' He glanced at his watch. 'You've had a long day and you need to get some more sleep now. Are you intending to work another early shift tomorrow?'

'Yes.' Tia nodded slowly, still trying to work out what she was going to do. She could ask him about Luisa, of course, but then she'd never know whether he would have told her himself given time.

'I'll take you to work,' he told her, the expression in his eyes suggesting that he wasn't going to take no for an answer.

'All right.' What choice did she have? Her bike was at the hospital.

His eyes narrowed. 'Now, go upstairs and relax in a warm bath. You need an early night or you'll be sick again.'

Too tired to argue, Tia slithered off the sofa and caught the blanket as it slipped to the floor.

'Are you planning to spend the night here again?'

'Of course.' His brows clashed in a frown, as if he was surprised that she should even ask the question. 'You're expecting my baby and you don't seem to be able to go through an entire day without vomiting and collapsing on me. There's no way I'm leaving you on your own.'

She stared at him, knowing that she should insist that he leave, but somehow unable to form the words. Having him in the cottage with her was strangely reassuring.

And unsettling.

'Well, if you're staying another night, you can use the spare room,' she said, knowing that she sounded ungracious but unable to help herself.

'Your generosity is overwhelming,' he drawled in response, but the corner of his firm mouth twitched slightly.

'I'll just remember not to stand up straight in the night or I'll be the one who's unconscious. The ceilings in this house are unbelievable. How tall is the average English man?'

Tia glanced at his powerful frame and then wished that she hadn't. There was nothing average about Luca Zattoni. He was overwhelmingly male, and aware of his own sexuality.

'Obviously the owner of this house wasn't very tall,' she said lamely, and he smiled. A slow, sexy grin that reminded her of all the reasons she'd fallen for him so heavily.

'Either that or he had a permanent headache. Goodnight, *cara*. Sleep well.'

Tia had trouble concentrating at work next day. All she could think about was Luca. He just seemed to take it for granted that their relationship would carry on.

'Is everything OK?' Sharon looked at her with concern. 'You're terribly pale, Tia.'

Tia summoned up a smile. She'd been sick again that morning but, fortunately for her, Luca had obviously still been asleep because this time she had the bathroom to herself.

'I'm fine,' she lied. 'Just a little tired. Where do you want me today?'

'On Postnatal for the time being. They're terribly busy, courtesy of all the deliveries yesterday.' Sharon moved closer and lowered her voice. 'Let's grab a coffee later if we get the chance.'

They didn't.

Tia didn't stop all morning, moving from one woman to another, performing daily checks and helping with feeding.

Fiona Adams was doing well and looking forward to going home.

'I'm just waiting for the paediatrician to come and check

Megan,' she told Tia with a smile. 'Then we're on our way.'

'That's great. And how's the feeding going?'

'Great. My milk has come in now and my boobs have trebled in size.' Fiona fished out an enormous bra from her bag and waved it at Tia. 'Look at that! Have you ever seen anything less sexy?'

Tia grinned. 'Well, it's not really designed to be sexy. It's designed to be practical and give you support.'

Mike, Fiona's husband, arrived at that moment, carrying a suitcase, and he laughed at the sight of the offending bra.

'You always said you wanted plastic surgery, love—now you know that all you needed was a baby.'

'All?' Fiona pretended to look offended. 'I'll have you know that your ''all'' kept me awake for most of the night. Did you bring the car seat?'

'Of course.' Mike looked at her patiently. 'Would I really have forgotten that? I couldn't carry everything at once, so it's still in the car.'

Fiona chewed her fingernails anxiously. 'It will be funny, being at home. Who will I talk to when I have a problem?'

'The community midwife will call until she's happy that you're fine and then there's the health visitor,' Tia told her, checking that she had all the telephone numbers. 'And if it's the middle of the night then you can always call us here.'

At that moment Megan woke up and started to yell.

'No!' Fiona stared at the baby, appalled. 'She can't possibly be hungry again! I've been feeding her for most of the night. She'll pop.'

'A breastfed baby doesn't always feed at regular times,' Tia reminded her, bending over the cot to scoop the baby up into her arms. 'Sometimes it might feel as though they're feeding non-stop, but don't forget that they regulate their own milk supply. The more they feed, the more you produce, so if she starts feeding a lot then you know that you're going to start making more for her.'

Fiona groaned. 'Well, there's no way I'm buying a bigger bra.'

'You can't. They don't come any bigger than that one,' Mike joked, his smile fading as he saw the expression on his wife's face. 'Sorry, sorry. You look great, love.'

Tia smiled and placed Megan gently in Fiona's arms. 'There you go.'

'Thanks.' Fiona's eyes misted. 'Look at that little nose.'

Mike bent over the pair of them and Tia made her excuses and left them in peace.

On her way out of the bay she bumped into Julie Douglas, the paediatric registrar.

'Baby Adams...?'

'In there...' Tia waved a hand. 'But they're having a SFM at the moment so I'd go and have a cup of tea.'

'SFM?' Julie looked blank and Sharon grinned as she sailed past.

'Soppy Family Moment. Definitely to be avoided,' she advised, grabbing Tia by the arm. 'Can you go and see how Dawn Henson is doing? The doctors are on their way round and last time I looked she was getting washed.'

Tia found Dawn back on her bed.

'How are you this morning?' She settled herself in the chair opposite and glanced into the cot. 'Fast asleep?'

Dawn rolled her eyes. 'At last. She's been awake virtually all night. If anyone wakes her up I'll strangle them with my bare hands.'

Tia grinned. 'That bad, huh?'

'How do mothers ever recover?' Dawn lay back against the pillows and closed her eyes. 'I'm shattered.'

Tia's smile faded. The woman did look tired. 'Tonight, why not ask the night staff to put her in the nursery for a few hours? They'll bring her to you when she needs feeding, but it just means that they'll settle her for you after the feed and you won't be woken by every snuffle.'

Dawn gave a wan smile. 'The trouble is, I'll be woken by everyone else's babies' snuffles. I've discovered that hospitals are not restful places.'

'That's true, but we can certainly give it a go.' Tia glanced up and felt her heart turn over as Luca strode down the ward with the rest of the team. 'I think the doctors want to take a look at you.'

Dawn struggled to sit up but Luca stopped her with a wave of his hand. 'Don't move. Just tell me how you feel.'

'All right, I suppose.' Dawn blushed slightly. 'A bit sore.'

Luca nodded and then questioned her quietly about her blood loss and asked if she'd had any pain.

Just as Dawn finished answering the baby woke and started to bawl.

'Oh, I don't believe it.' Dawn gave a horrified groan. 'I'd only just got her off. She can't be hungry.'

'Perhaps she just needs a hug?' Luca lifted an eyebrow towards Dawn, seeking permission to pick the baby up, and she nodded.

'Be my guest. I think my arms are too tired to hold her.'

Luca scooped the bawling bundle up carefully and tucked her expertly on his shoulder.

'Did you hear your mama?' His voice was deep and gentle as he spoke to the baby. 'She says that you cannot possibly be hungry, so maybe you just had a bad dream, hmm?'

Ignoring the rest of his colleagues, who were looking at him in amazement, he switched to Italian and talked quietly to the baby, his voice softening as the baby's eyes started to close again.

Within moments the baby was asleep again, lulled by his deep voice and the soothing touch of his hands.

Carefully he laid her back in the cot and smiled at the mother. 'Hopefully you can now have five minutes' peace.'

Dawn was wide eyed with amazement. 'How did you do that? Thank you.'

'Prego.' Luca inclined his head and then issued some instructions to Dr Ford who was looking as elegant as ever.

Tia watched them move on to the next patient and held back a sigh.

'He is truly gorgeous,' Dawn muttered, shifting herself into a more comfortable position. 'I tell you, I would have swapped places with my daughter if I could! I wonder what it would be like to have a man like that run his hands over you and speak to you in Italian.'

Tia stared after Luca's broad shoulders and felt her insides twist.

She knew exactly what it felt like.

Incredible.

'Tia?' Julie walked up, stethoscope looped around her neck. 'I've checked baby Adams and she's fine. As far as I'm concerned, they can go home.'

'Thanks.' Tia pulled herself together and went to check that Fiona was all set for her discharge.

She was, and she and Mike gazed proudly at their daughter, safely strapped in her new car seat.

'She looks so tiny in that.' Fiona's voice wobbled slightly and Mike gave her shoulder a squeeze.

'Yeah, and in no time she's going to be nagging you for make-up and trendy clothes, so make the most of it. At least at this age they don't run up a phone bill.'

Tia walked down the corridor with them and waited while they climbed into the lift.

'Are you off, Fiona?' Sharon bustled up and said her goodbyes and then grabbed Tia by the arm. 'Kettle's boiled.'

* * *

'What am I going to do?' Tia stared at her friend helplessly. 'He wants us to spend time together and get to know each other.'

Sharon spooned sugar into her coffee and stirred it thoughtfully. 'I'd say that's a good idea.' She dropped the spoon into an empty mug and picked up her coffee. 'Tia, you're crazy about the man. Stop looking for problems. Whatever did—or didn't—happen with Luisa, he's clearly chosen you. Accept that and move on.'

'But I don't know whether he's just chosen me because of the baby.'

'So ask him,' Sharon suggested. 'Maybe it's time you were honest. Tell him what you heard about Luisa and see what he says.'

'No,' Tia said flatly. 'If I have to ask him, I'll never be able to trust him again. He has to tell me himself.'

Sharon sighed. 'Tia, not everyone is a rat like your father.'

'No?' Tia's eyes were suddenly overly bright. 'But how do I know for sure? I don't find it easy to trust men.'

'I know that.' Sharon gave a wry smile. 'I didn't think that you'd ever get married—' She broke off and flushed, suddenly realising what she'd said. 'Not that you did, of course, but you nearly did—'

'Before I realised what a complete fool I was being.'

'You weren't being a fool,' Sharon said firmly. 'You love Luca, Tia.'

'Do I?' Tia closed her eyes for a second. 'Do you know, I'm not even sure of that any more.'

Sharon looked perplexed. 'Well, how does he make you feel when you're with him?'

'I don't know.' Tia shook her head. 'Breathless. Confused. Dizzy. Sick. Excited.'

Desperate.

Desperate for him to drag her into his arms and make love to her.

'To be honest, he has such a powerful effect on me physically that I can't work out how I feel about him,' Tia admitted finally. 'It's like being a teenager again. If he's even in the same room as me I feel weak.'

Sharon gave a smug, self-satisfied grin. 'You see? I always said it would happen like that for you. I always said that you'd be swept off your feet if you found the right man.'

The right man.

Was that Luca?

She'd certainly thought that he was but now, after everything that had happened, she wasn't so sure.

'How do you tell the difference between lust and love?'

Sharon pursed her lips thoughtfully and stared into her drink. 'Well, I suppose the answer to that is that you take lust out of the equation.'

'What do you mean?'

'You do what he says. Literally.' Sharon gave a little shrug. 'You get to know each other properly. You know, talking, long walks, laughter, dinner. But no bed.'

'No bed?' Tia looked at her stupidly and Sharon grinned.

'Tough one, huh? Personally I can't imagine living with a man like Luca and having no bed, but I suppose it does make sense in a sort of twisted way. It seems to me that all you've shared so far is passion and none of the other things that you share when you're developing a relationship with someone. Maybe if you knew him better you'd know whether he was the sort of person likely to have an affair.'

'It isn't always stamped on a man's forehead, you know,' Tia mumbled. 'My poor mother thought my father loved her, was faithful, and then—'

'Yes,' Sharon interrupted her quickly, 'but let's not think about that now. You're not throwing away the chance of a relationship with a man like Luca just because your father was less than perfect.'

'But—'

'Just give it a go, Tia,' Sharon advised. 'What have you

got to lose? If you decide that it isn't going to work, that you really can't trust him, then go your separate ways. You won't be any worse off for giving it a try.'

Tia stared at her. Wouldn't she?

Maybe Sharon was right. On the other hand, she had an uncomfortable feeling that the more time she spent with Luca, the harder it would be to let him go.

'But we're so different, Shaz,' she said simply. 'Even forgetting about the Luisa thing, we're different. For a start, he hates me working and you know that I need to work.'

'I think once he gets to know you, he'll understand why you need to work.' Sharon's face was suddenly serious. 'You say that you don't really know him, but how much does he really know about you?'

Tia felt her heart flutter in her chest. 'Probably not very much.'

Sharon nodded slowly. 'It strikes me that the pair of you have got too many secrets. Have you told him that you've always been scared of having children?'

'Hardly.' Tia gripped her mug tightly. 'He's Italian, Shaz,' she croaked. 'Italian men love children. How can I possibly tell him that I'm terrified of being a mother?'

'I think what's important is that you're honest with each other, and I really think that you need to tell him what you heard his mother and Luisa saying the day of your wedding.'

'No.' Tia shook her head stubbornly. 'Definitely not that. That is something that he needs to tell me himself.'

But would he?

CHAPTER FOUR

'YOU'RE very quiet,' Luca observed as he drove them both home. 'Are you upset?'

Upset and confused.

Tia glanced sideways at him and then wished she hadn't. Every time she looked at his mouth her stomach swooped in the direction of her shoes and she felt an almost desperate need for him to kiss her as only he could.

'This whole situation is such a mess,' she muttered, rubbing slim fingers over her forehead to ease the tension. 'We don't know each other, Luca.'

Luca's gaze didn't leave the road. 'And there is a simple solution to that, as we have already agreed. We get to know each other.' He turned into the lane that led to the cottage, pulled up and switched the engine off. 'Have you considered what I proposed earlier?'

The smooth Italian accent was enough to melt a polar icecap and she felt her heart start to beat faster. It had always been like that with Luca. One look, one word had been all it took to set her on fire. He hadn't actually needed to touch her to get a reaction, but when he had...

But could there really be more between them than a breathtakingly powerful attraction?

Or was Luisa the woman he really wanted?

'I—I don't know, Luca,' she said finally, her head starting to throb with the stress of the situation.

He nodded slowly. 'You are treating this like a major life decision, but perhaps you should look at it another way,' he suggested, his voice calm and level. 'Already you are expecting our baby. You owe it to our family to take some time to make this relationship work.'

Our family.

Tia felt a lump building in her throat. He made it sound simple and straightforward but, of course, it wasn't.

Living together as a family meant living with Luca—having him close to her all the time.

It would be torture.

'Why are you hesitating?' His voice was velvety smooth and she closed her eyes and gave a wry smile.

'Because the one word we haven't mentioned is love, that's why.' What he was describing sounded more like a business arrangement.

'Love...' Something flickered briefly in his dark eyes and then it was gone. 'Just because our feelings for each other aren't what they might be, it doesn't mean we can't live together amicably and create a stable family for our child.'

A stable family.

For a brief moment Tia's mind flitted back to her own childhood and in that instant she made her decision.

'All right.' She turned to face him, her mind made up. 'We'll do as you suggest and get to know each other better, but there are two conditions on my part.'

Luca's smooth brows twitched into a frown. He clearly hadn't been expecting conditions. 'Which are?'

She felt her heart thumping madly. 'Firstly, that you accept the fact that I want to work. No disapproving looks, no arguments, no atmosphere when I leave the house in the morning and end up working extra hours.'

His jaw tightened and his stunning eyes narrowed. 'And second?'

'Second.' She swallowed hard and looked away from him, bracing herself for his reaction. 'Second is no touching.'

A long silence stretched between them and eventually he spoke, his voice lethally soft. *'Excuse me?'*

Her eyes slid to his incredulous dark gaze and she took a deep breath.

'No touching. I can't think straight when you touch me, Luca,' she said, the words tumbling out in a rush as she tried to explain herself. He was well aware of the effect he had on her physically so there was no point in being anything but honest. 'It's the reason we're in this mess right now. We need to find out whether we truly like each other and we can't do that if we're physically close. You can live in the same house as me but you sleep in the spare room.'

There was an ominous silence which stretched on and on. When he finally spoke his voice was raw.

'You are seriously suggesting that we live together but don't make love?'

Her heart was now thumping so hard she thought it might explode through her chest.

'Yes.' Considering the state of her insides, her voice was surprisingly steady. 'It makes sense, Luca.'

There was another long silence and she grew steadily more uncomfortable under his incredulous gaze. She realised now that she'd been ridiculously naïve to even think that a man as physical as Luca would agree to such a condition.

'All right.'

She gaped at him, wondering if she'd misheard. 'Luca…'

'If that is what you want, then we'll do it.'

Tia swallowed.

What she wanted…

She'd thought it was what she wanted but looking at his powerful shoulders and smouldering dark gaze she was beginning to think she must be slightly mad. What woman would ask a man like Luca *not* to touch her?

And she couldn't believe that he'd agreed to it. She shot him a suspicious look but his expression was unreadable. If he had another agenda then he was keeping it well hidden.

'And you won't make a fuss about me working?'

His mouth compressed. 'As long as you agree to restrict the hours you do and to let me buy you a car.'

She frowned. 'I don't need a car.'

'A car,' he interrupted her, his gaze steely, 'or you don't work.'

She could see that he wasn't going to give an inch and she gave a sigh. 'All right. Thank you. A car. But a small car.'

'*A small car?*' The tension seemed to leave him and his eyes shimmered with amusement. 'You are the first woman I have ever met who would choose to have a small car. The rest of your sex would be handing me brochures of glamorous sports cars at this point.'

His smile made her heart flip over. 'I don't want a glamorous sports car,' she told him. 'It's a waste of money.'

'Indeed.' His tone was dry and a smile flickered across his handsome face. 'Now, onto your second condition. No touching.'

The car suddenly seemed a very confined space and he suddenly seemed very, very male.

'It's true that the physical attraction between us is unusually strong.' His eyes dropped to her mouth and then lifted again to her wide green eyes. 'I can see how it has possibly overwhelmed other aspects of our relationship, so I agree to your second condition. No touching.' The corner of his mouth lifted slightly. 'Although I have a feeling it may not be easy.'

Tia gave a weak smile. She had a feeling that it wouldn't be easy either. Heavens, even now she was dying for the man to kiss her. It wouldn't be so bad if she didn't already know just what he could make her feel. But she did...

Luca touched her cheek gently and pulled the key out of the ignition. 'But any time you want to change that rule, let me know.'

He opened his door and she watched him unfold his six-foot-plus frame, her heart beating a steady tattoo against her chest.

Change the rule?

His straightforward admission that he still wanted her made her limbs tremble.

Not that wanting her physically meant anything, of course. Luca had already proved that he didn't need to be in love with her to enjoy an intense physical relationship.

But that wasn't enough for her.

She was going to get to know him, and then decide what the future held for them.

The following morning Luca took her to work without comment, although she could see from the stiff line of his jaw that he wasn't pleased with the idea.

'I'll be OK, Luca,' she said quietly as she undid her seat belt and fumbled for her bag. 'I wasn't sick this morning.'

He turned to her, his eyes serious. 'Tia, I'm not happy about you working, you know that. There is no financial reason for you to work and I don't really understand why you feel the need, but I gave you my word and I won't try and stop you. But if you are unwell, I want you to call me. Do you understand?'

She hesitated and then gave a nod. 'All right, but I think you're overreacting.'

'I'm Italian and an expectant father,' he pointed out, a smile touching his firm mouth. 'I'm allowed to overreact.'

Unable to resist the lazy warmth in his eyes she returned the smile, remembering that it had been his sense of humour that had first attracted her to him. That and his aura of strength.

'We still haven't really talked about this baby, Tia,' he pointed out softly as he parked and switched off the engine. 'Tonight I'll make us some dinner and we can discuss it properly. You wanted us to get to know each other better, so our feelings about the baby are a good place to start.'

Her heart gave a lurch. She wasn't at all sure that she was ready to discuss how she felt about the baby.

She had little chance to think about it, however, because Sharon grabbed her the minute she arrived on the unit.

'I need you on Antenatal. We've had an emergency admission from A and E.' She matched her pace to Tia's as they walked quickly along the corridor, talking as they went. 'They thought she had some sort of viral illness to start with, but now they think it's severe pre-eclampsia.'

Luca was at the desk, together with Dr Ford and Dan Sutherland, the consultant.

'She complained of severe headache and visual disturbances,' Luca was telling the team, 'and she's also had epigastric pain and vomiting. The casualty officer thought it was a virus to start with but was smart enough to do a pregnancy test.'

'She didn't know she was pregnant?' Dr Ford looked slightly disdainful and Luca flashed her a slightly impatient look.

'It would seem not.'

Dan Sutherland picked up the notes. 'Does she have many risk factors for pre-eclampsia?'

'A few.' Luca raked long fingers through his dark hair. 'First baby, overweight, family history according to the case officer—her mother had pre-eclampsia—and her blood pressure was already high.'

Dan frowned. 'How do we know that?'

'The casualty officer rang the GP to check on her history.'

Dan raised his eyebrows in surprise. 'Smart chap.'

Luca gave a wry smile. 'It was a woman,' he drawled softly, his eyes flickering back to the notes. 'She called me down to A and E because she was worried, I examined the patient and gave her a nifedipine capsule to chew because we needed something fast-acting. In my opinion she was—

and is—at very high risk of developing full-blown eclampsia.'

Dan nodded. 'All right, let's take a look at her. She's going to need one-to-one care, I should think.'

'Tia will be her midwife,' Sharon said quickly, pushing open the door and holding it while they all trooped into the room.

'Hello, Sue, I'm Dan Sutherland, the consultant and this is Dr Zattoni, my senior registrar, and Dr Ford...' Dan made the introductions as Sue Gibbs lay on the bed, clearly very ill. 'And you had no idea you were pregnant?'

Sue shook her head, slowly. 'None. My husband and I were desperate to have a baby, but in the end nothing happened so we gave up. I still can't believe I'm pregnant. Are you absolutely sure?'

Dan gave a brief nod. 'But it seems that you've developed a condition called pre-eclampsia, Sue. Which is basically high blood pressure of pregnancy. It can be dangerous if not controlled, so we're trying to bring your blood pressure down.'

'Will the baby be all right?'

'Don't worry about the baby,' Dan said immediately. 'The scan shows us that at the moment he's fine. His heartbeat is strong and he's still moving around. It's you we need to worry about.'

He motioned to Tia to take over with the patient and moved to one side with Luca.

'We need to give her an anti-hypertensive by infusion, do you agree?'

Luca nodded. 'And we need to catheterise her and monitor her output.'

Dan cast another look at the patient and then lowered his voice. 'I suggest you stay close.'

Luca nodded, understanding immediately. 'That was my intention.' He turned to Dr Ford. 'I want you to check U and Es, LFTs, urate and placental function and platelets. A falling platelet count and changes in clotting factors have been reported in many cases of pre-eclampsia. Tia, can you put her on a monitor and keep her on it for now?'

Tia nodded. It was obvious that they were very worried about Sue.

She monitored Sue's blood pressure regularly throughout the morning but despite the drugs it still crept upwards.

She slipped out of the room briefly to have a word with Luca, who was at the desk finishing a telephone call, Dr Ford by his side.

'Her blood pressure is sneaking up again,' she mouthed, and he nodded as he replaced the receiver.

'She is at a very high risk of developing full-blown eclampsia,' he agreed and Dr Ford frowned.

'But you've given her anti-hypertensives.'

'Anti-hypertensives do not alter the course of pre-eclampsia,' Luca reminded her. 'There is only one thing that will do that, which is?'

He paused, waiting for Dr Ford to answer, but she looked at him blankly.

'Delivery.' Tia broke the awkward silence, thinking that if the glamorous Dr Ford paid as much attention to her textbooks as she did to her make-up and her male colleagues, she might be a better doctor.

'Yes.' There was a warmth in Luca's eyes as they rested on her briefly and then he turned his attention back to his SHO. 'I'd like you to bleep Duncan Fraser, the anaesthetist, and warn him that we might need his services at short notice, and do the same with Paeds, please. I think we're probably going to need to get the baby out. And could you also call ITU and check their bed state?'

Dr Ford reached for the phone, her expression flustered for the first time.

Tia followed Luca back to the room.

Sue's husband, Eddie, was sitting on the bed, his face ashen.

'Will she be all right?'

'She is very ill,' Luca said honestly, 'but she is in the right place and we are doing everything we can.'

Eddie's face crumpled and Luca put a sympathetic hand on his shoulder. 'Come with me to the relatives' room,' he said quietly, 'and I can explain exactly what is happening.'

They left the room and Tia was alone with Sue.

She checked her patient's blood pressure again and then tensed. As she watched, Sue became suddenly restless, her head drawn to one side, then her body went into spasm and she started to fit.

'Damn!' Smashing her hand against the emergency button, Tia immediately inserted an airway, quickly disconnected the CTG machine and shifted Sue into a semi-prone position.

Grabbing the oxygen, she placed the mask over Sue's face, knowing that care of the mother was everything.

She heard footsteps outside the door and sighed with relief.

Reinforcements...

Luca came back into the room at a run, his eyes taking in the problem immediately.

'I want to give her magnesium sulphate,' he ordered, his voice calm and level as he delivered his instructions. 'Give her 4 g in 100 ml of normal saline over at least five minutes, and then I want an infusion rate of 1 g an hour for 24 hours.'

Tia prepared the drug and gave it to Luca to check.

'All right.' He gave the drug and glanced towards Dr Ford. 'Check her patellar reflexes every fifteen minutes. Tia, her resps should be more than sixteen a minute. Check every fifteen minutes and if it drops below that I want to know immediately. And let's keep an eye on her urine output.'

Duncan Fraser, the anaesthetist, hurried into the room at that point and Luca glanced up, his expression grim.

'We need to section her now.'

Duncan nodded. 'Let's get on with it, then.'

It was the fastest section Tia had ever seen, and in no time the baby was out and screaming with outrage.

'Sounds hopeful,' Luca commented, his eyes still on the wound. 'Julie? Give me some good news on the baby.'

'He seems fine.' Julie Douglas, the paediatric registrar, had the baby on the rescusitaire and was checking it over. 'Small, of course—I've warned Special Care to expect a new customer. How's Mum?'

'Not good.' Luca didn't look up. 'Someone, please, tell Eddie that he has a little boy. The man must be out of his mind with worry. Tia, can you do that?'

'Of course.'

Tia checked again that the baby seemed all right and then walked into the anteroom where Eddie was pacing, frantic with worry.

'Eddie, you have a baby boy,' Tia said softly, and he stared at her, ashen-faced and stunned.

'A boy?' He looked at her stupidly and then shook his head, rubbing a hand around the back of his neck to relieve the tension. 'Ridiculous, isn't it? We always wanted a baby, and now we've got one I don't really care. All I want is for Sue to be back to normal. How is she?'

'She's poorly,' Tia admitted, 'but she's getting the best possible care. Dr Zattoni is just finishing in Theatre and then she'll be transferred to ITU. You can go and see her when they've settled her down.'

'And the—my son?'

'He's beautiful.' Tia smiled at him. 'Very small, so he'll be in Special Care for now. The paediatrician is taking him up there now. Are you ready to see him?'

Eddie licked his lips. 'I don't know.'

Suddenly Tia made a decision. 'Wait there.'

She slipped back into Theatre and walked quickly up to

Julie. 'Can I take the baby for two minutes? If we wrap him up well…'

Julie stared at her. 'You want to take the baby?'

'His father doesn't know whether he's coming or going,' Tia told her quickly. 'I think he needs to see his little boy quickly. Just for a moment.'

Julie frowned. 'But—'

'Julie, will it harm the baby if he is well wrapped up for a few minutes?' Luca's voice intervened across the theatre. 'I agree with Tia that it is important. This family have had a terrible shock—they are not prepared for this baby at all. If we're not careful, we could have bonding problems.'

His dark eyes locked with Tia's and she knew what he was thinking.

If Sue died, would Eddie blame the child?

'It should be all right, I suppose.' Julie gave a nod and wrapped the baby, handing him carefully to Tia. 'Don't be long. He needs to be checked out in Special Care.'

'Hello, sweetheart.' Tia gazed down at the tiny features of the baby and her heart melted. He looked completely helpless. 'We're going to meet your daddy, so be a good boy and don't let me down.'

Someone opened the door to the anteroom for her and she slipped inside and walked across to Eddie who was sitting with his head in his hands.

'Someone to meet you, Eddie.' Taking a chance that her instincts were correct, she laid the tiny bundle on his lap and held her breath.

There was a long silence. Eddie stared wordlessly down at his baby son and then tears started to pour down his cheeks.

'He's beautiful,' he croaked, tightening his grip on the little bundle. 'So beautiful. How can I possibly blame anything so perfect? I still can't take it all in—we thought we couldn't have children.'

He rambled incoherently for a few minutes and Tia slipped an arm around his shoulder.

'He's beautiful, Eddie,' Tia said softly, feeling her own eyes fill as she watched him. 'A bit small, but the paediatrician thinks he's doing very well. I don't suppose you've thought of a name?'

'Oh, yes.' Eddie gave an embarrassed sniff and gazed down at his son. 'We always knew what we'd call a little boy. Harry.'

'That's lovely.' Tia's voice cracked and she cleared her throat. Maybe being pregnant made her more emotional than usual. 'OK, well, we need to get Harry up to the ward now...'

Julie was hovering in the doorway, keeping a close eye on her charge. 'Why don't you come, too, Mr Gibbs? You can stay with him while we settle him in and then go and tell your wife all about him.'

It was hours later when they finally climbed into Luca's car to drive home.

'I can't believe how quickly she fitted,' Luca said as he reversed the car out of his space. 'You had an airway in the room, ready? That was quick thinking.'

'In my pocket,' Tia murmured. 'It seemed like a good idea.'

'It was more than a good idea.' Luca flicked the indicator and pulled onto the main road. 'You're an excellent midwife. How on earth did you manage to put her in the recovery position by yourself?'

Tia shrugged. 'Panic, I suppose. I kept thinking that if Sue died, the baby would die, too.' She gave a sigh. 'Do you think she will die, Luca?'

He pulled a face. 'I don't know. She is certainly very sick but I hope that she will be all right.'

'You were fantastic,' Tia said softly, a flush touching her cheeks. 'Really fantastic.'

He glanced at her briefly and his gaze burned into hers. 'Thank you.'

They arrived at the cottage and Luca pushed open the door. 'What a day! Go and have a bath and I'll prepare supper.'

She stifled a grin. 'Another omelette?'

'No.' He shut the front door behind them and walked through to the kitchen. 'I'm the first to admit that my experience in the kitchen is limited but I arranged to have some shopping delivered today so there should be something simple in the fridge.'

She stared at him. 'You went shopping?'

Luca Zattoni? *Shopping?*

He gave a shake of his head and a wry smile. 'No. I didn't exactly go shopping. But I arranged for the supermarket to deliver.'

She blinked at him. 'What supermarket? And how could they deliver? We weren't in.'

A flush touched his hard cheekbones. 'Dan Sutherland's secretary ordered everything and I gave her a key to the cottage. She nipped here today so that someone was in when they delivered.'

Luca had arranged all that? The least domesticated male on the planet?

Tia was totally speechless and he gave her a gentle push. 'Go and have a bath.'

Without argument she wandered upstairs and minutes later she slid into a deep bubble bath with a contented sigh. She still couldn't believe that Luca had really gone to those lengths just for her. It was totally out of character.

Or maybe it wasn't.

Maybe it was just another indication that she didn't really know much about him.

Drifting away with her thoughts, she was still trying to make sense of it when the door opened ten minutes later.

Tia gave a squeak of embarrassment and slid under the bubbles as Luca strolled in.

'What are you doing? You promised—'

'I promised I wouldn't touch you,' Luca drawled softly, his eyes darkening as they rested on the gentle swell of her breasts. 'And I haven't.'

Not with his hands maybe, but with his eyes…

'I knocked, but you didn't answer. I wanted to check that you hadn't fallen asleep in the bath.'

'Well, I haven't,' Tia muttered, and he gave a slow smile.

'In that case, why don't you get dried and come down to supper?'

Not while he was standing there!

Suddenly she was hideously aware of every inch of her naked body and her eyes meshed with his. Oh, dear God, how had she ever thought she'd be able to keep the physical element out of their relationship?

He'd removed his jacket and undone his top button and she could see a hint of dark, curling chest hair at the top of his shirt. And she could remember exactly how his chest looked. How it felt under her eager fingers. The way his muscles curved, strong and sleek, and the way his body hair trailed downwards…

She swallowed and slid further under the water. She needed a cold shower, not a hot bath.

He handed her a towel and from the gleam in his eyes she was fairly sure that he knew exactly what she was thinking.

Damn the man.

How was she going to get dressed and eat supper without breaking her own rules? She was desperate for him to touch her.

But she'd made the rules and now she had to stick to them. No touching, she'd said, and he'd agreed.

It was going to be a difficult evening.

CHAPTER FIVE

WHEN Tia finally plucked up the courage to slink into the kitchen, she was amazed by what she saw.

Instead of relying on the usual harsh kitchen lights, Luca had found some candles and grouped them in the centre of the scrubbed pine table. The subtle, cosy lighting flickered across the room, revealing a tempting selection of mouth-watering dishes which he'd laid out on the table.

The atmosphere was romantic and intimate and she felt inexplicably shy. She really didn't know this man at all. It was like being with a stranger. The longer she knew him, the more he surprised her.

'I thought all you could cook was omelette?' She used humour to try and disguise just how confused she was feeling, and he returned the smile as he strolled across the room towards her.

'I haven't exactly cooked,' he confessed, glancing at the table with a wry smile. 'And we both know that my omelette was inedible.'

Another point in his favour. He obviously had no problem admitting when he wasn't good at something.

'Well, this looks fantastic.' There was a delicious-smelling soup, crusty bread and various cold meats and salads. Her smile was teasing. 'For an unreconstructed Italian male, you're obviously good in the kitchen.'

'I am very good in the kitchen, *cara mia.*' Suddenly the temperature of the room seemed to shoot up and his eyes gleamed wickedly. 'And so are you, if my memory is correct.'

'Luca, for goodness' sake...' She blushed deeply but couldn't look away from his compelling gaze.

'I was late home from work and I'd ruined your dinner.' His soft voice caressed her nerve endings. 'Do you remember that night, Tia?'

Of course she remembered that night.

The minute he'd walked through the door their dinner had been forgotten.

'Luca...' His name was almost a plea on her lips and she felt sexual heat curl deep inside her stomach.

He slid a hand behind her head and gently forced her to look at him. 'It has always been like that between us, has it not?' His voice was husky with desire and his eyes slid to her mouth.

For endless seconds they stood still, both battling against the physical force which drew them together, then Luca released her suddenly and stalked to the other side of the kitchen.

'I must have been mad to agree to the no-touching rule.' His voice was a frustrated growl and he dragged both hands through his black hair, his eyes stormy. 'Maybe I should check into a hotel until we decide that our relationship can move forward.'

Tia felt her heart lurch uncomfortably in her chest. Would it move forward? She wasn't sure.

'We were supposed to spend the evening talking,' she reminded him, a small smile of satisfaction touching her mouth as she registered his tension.

It was good to know that, physically at least, he wanted her as much as she wanted him.

'Talking.' The corner of his mouth quirked and he shrugged his broad shoulders. 'OK. Maybe if you sit at one end of the table and I sit at the other...'

Tia slid into a chair and concentrated on the food. Suddenly talking didn't seem as easy as it had sounded. She could barely keep her body functioning properly when she was in the same room as the man, let alone hold a conversation. She wanted Luca so much it was a physical ache.

'What shall we talk about?' Her voice came out as a squeak and she cursed herself as she read the gleam in his eyes. He was totally aware of the effect he had on her.

'You.' He leaned back in his chair at the opposite end of the table, thick, dark lashes shielding his expression as he watched her. 'You are a very private person, Tia. I want to know more about you. A great deal more.'

His speculative dark gaze made her feel like a dizzy teenager. 'There's not much to know,' she hedged, and he gave a short laugh.

'Tia, we are both in agreement that we have spent insufficient time talking. For example, I know nothing about your family. All you told me was that your parents died when you were young. Do you have no other family?'

She played with her soup self-consciously.

She really wasn't used to talking about her childhood.

'No.' She scrabbled in her mind for a change of subject. 'Unlike you, who are surrounded by family.'

He inclined his head in agreement, a rueful smile touching his firm mouth. 'A mixed blessing, as you've discovered.'

Tia glanced at him. 'I bet they're not too pleased that you've chased me to England.'

He gave a careless shrug. 'I have no idea what they think. I'm not in the habit of seeking their approval. My father died when I was twelve and I've been making my own decisions ever since.'

She stared at him, beginning to understand why he was so self-assured.

'I'm sorry,' she said quietly. 'That must have been difficult for you. How did he die?'

'Living life to the full,' Luca said wryly, his voice amazingly matter-of-fact as he described an event that must have had devastating consequences for a young boy. 'He was riding a motorbike. My mother thought that my father took too many risks for a man with children, and maybe he did…' He shrugged. 'I don't know. Fortunately his business was thriving and my uncles were able to carry on running it so she had no financial worries, but my mother had always let my father make all the decisions and suddenly he was gone.'

'So you took over?'

He nodded slowly. 'I was barely more than a child myself, but that's exactly what I did and soon everyone expected me to make decisions for them.'

Tia tilted her head on one side, a smile touching her mouth. 'Are you trying to justify why you're so autocratic?'

'No. That's probably just a basic character flaw.' He gave an apologetic smile that was so sexy it made her stomach flip. He really was staggeringly handsome.

'But you made all the decisions in the family?'

He gave a dismissive shrug. 'I suppose so.'

Tia nodded. 'Well that explains a lot about you.'

'It does?' His dark eyes shimmered with amusement and she blushed.

'Well, if you're used to bossing your sisters and your mother then I suppose it's hardly surprising that you try and take over my life, too,' she said quickly, hoping that he couldn't read her mind. Her thoughts were positively X-rated! 'The trouble is, I've also been looking after myself since I was young and I don't need anyone to make decisions for me. It's probably why we clash.'

Luca's gaze sharpened. 'How young?'

She played idly with her knife. 'Eight.'

'Eight years old?' His voice was soft. 'That must have been very hard, *cara mia*.'

She gave a dismissive shrug. 'Maybe.'

He sighed and sat back in his chair. 'Tia, I'm fully aware that you change the subject every time I mention your parents.' His voice was gentle. 'Are you going to hide from me for ever, or are you going to trust me?'

There was a lengthy silence. He was right, of course.

She *did* hide from people and she always had. It was a defence mechanism that she'd developed over the years. And as for trusting him...

'Tia, if you want me to understand you, you have to start revealing some of yourself to me,' he said quietly, and she swallowed hard, acknowledging the truth of what he was saying.

'My parents were actors,' she said, quickly outlining the bare facts. 'They married very young—too young, I suppose. My mother was crazy about my father and she thought that he felt the same way about her.'

Luca's eyes were fixed on her face. 'But he didn't?'

Tia's mouth tightened. 'It would seem not. He had one affair after another and my mother started to drink. Too much.' She broke off and glanced at him briefly. 'She died when I was eight.'

He let out a long breath. 'And your father?'

Tia played with her spoon. 'My father made it clear that he couldn't look after me so I went into care.'

'Care?' He looked blank. 'You stayed with family?'

'There was no family,' Tia said simply. 'I went into foster-care and then a children's home while I waited for someone to adopt me. But they didn't.' She gave an overly bright smile. 'And who can blame them? You think I'm reckless now, you should have met me then. I was your average teenage nightmare.'

His gaze didn't falter and she knew that her bravado hadn't fooled him. 'So you never had a proper home? Family?'

'No.'

'That must have been difficult.' His voice was even, as if he knew that too much sympathy would be hard to cope with.

She stirred her soup slowly. 'Well, it made me very independent. It's probably the reason I don't take kindly to people telling me what to do,' she told him with a smile.

'I'm used to having to work things out for myself because I've always been on my own.'

'But you're not on your own now.'

She lifted her eyes to his and her heart squeezed tightly at the expression in his eyes.

'No…'

'But you are finding it hard, are you not,' he said calmly, 'to learn to trust another person? Presumably because of what happened to your mother and because you have been let down so many times in the past.'

'Yes,' she said honestly. 'I—I didn't think I'd ever be able to trust a man. Even now I'm worried that you—that you…' Her eyes slid away from his and she stumbled slightly over the words. 'Might be keeping all sorts of secrets from me.'

There—she'd said it. Now she just had to wait for Luca's response.

She looked at him, searching for signs of guilt or discomfort but she saw nothing but sympathy in his expression.

'Tia, you can trust me,' he said quietly, his dark eyes trapping hers 'But I can understand that, with your experiences, my word is not enough to stop you worrying. Only time will do that. So let us tackle another issue. How do you feel about being pregnant? How do you feel about having my baby?'

Her heart thumped steadily as she looked into his eyes. Could she tell him the truth? That she was terrified? That she wasn't sure she'd be a good mother.

No.

She couldn't threaten the fragile peace that had settled between them by admitting that she'd never thought she'd get married or have children.

'I'm pleased about the baby,' she whispered at last, concentrating her attentions on the plate of ham in front of her. 'Very pleased.'

There was a long silence and she could feel his gaze sweeping her pale face.

'Are you sure? This isn't the time for secrets between us. I want you to tell me the truth.'

Secrets?

He was a fine one to talk about secrets when he still hadn't mentioned Luisa.

'I'm pleased,' she repeated firmly, poking at her food. 'What about you, Luca? How do you really feel now that you've had time to get used to the idea?'

'I still would have chosen to have more time alone with you,' he admitted, his accent almost unbearably sexy, 'especially in the light of what you've just told me, but I am very pleased, Tia. Very pleased indeed. I love children.'

Tia added some salad to her plate, her hands shaking slightly. Of course he loved children. All Italian men loved children, didn't they?

'But if I hadn't got pregnant? What then?'

He shrugged. 'Then we would have had more time to get to know each other properly. But it is pointless to dwell on what might have happened. We need to concentrate on the present. You still haven't seen a doctor. I want you to register with Dan.'

She opened her mouth to accuse him of being autocratic but then closed it again. Luca was right. Dan was easily the best consultant. Everyone knew it. And he was kind and approachable too. *Which helped when you were absolutely terrified.*

'I'll talk to him,' she offered, and Luca lifted an ebony brow.

'Just like that.' His mouth twitched at the corners. 'No arguments? No accusations of trying to run your life?'

'It just so happens that on this occasion I agree with you, that's all,' she said primly, and he laughed.

'Well, that is definitely a first. Maybe we're making progress.'

Maybe they were.

The next morning she was sick again and Luca was by her side in an instant. He murmured something soothing in Italian and held her until she finally collapsed against him, exhausted.

'Oh, Luca.' She felt pitifully sorry for herself and he tightened his grip.

'Remind me to be more sympathetic the next time a woman tells me she is suffering from morning sickness,' he said gruffly, wiping her face with a flannel and helping her to her feet. 'I never realised how awful it can be. Go back to bed for a few minutes and I'll bring you a drink.'

She did as she was told, knowing that she shouldn't be leaning on him but unable to help herself. She had to admit that for a very macho male, he was surprisingly undaunted by her antics in the bathroom.

He walked back into the room and she noticed for the first time that he was wearing nothing but a pair of loose-fitting tracksuit bottoms.

'I was still in bed when I heard you get up,' he said, intercepting her look and proffering an explanation. 'I'm not in the habit of wearing clothes to bed.'

She was well aware of that and the sight of his tanned, muscular chest was a tantalising reminder of what the rest of him looked like.

Incredible...

He had the perfect musculature of an athlete and she averted her eyes and took the glass of water he brought her with a murmur of thanks.

The bed sagged slightly under his weight as he sat down next to her. 'I don't suppose there's any chance I can persuade you not to work today?'

'None at all,' she said, putting the glass of water back on the bedside table. 'I feel much better now.'

'Right.' Luca rolled his eyes and gave a wry smile. 'Has anyone ever told you that you're difficult to handle?'

'Yes. Lots of times.' Tia swung her legs out of bed and reached for her dressing-gown, taking deep breaths to calm her stomach. 'Now, if you'll excuse me, I'm going to use the bathroom. Hopefully to wash this time.' She walked towards the door, deliberately avoiding looking at the powerful muscles of his shoulders.

The no-touching rule was becoming harder by the minute.

Luca drove her to the hospital and Tia found herself working in the antenatal clinic for the morning.

'Do you mind, Tia?' Sharon immediately apologised. 'I'm moving you around everywhere, I know, but I've got a midwife off sick and we've got a busy clinic. You should enjoy it—your Luca's working down there this morning.'

He was?

Tia's heart lurched uncomfortably. On the one hand, concentrating was difficult with Luca around but, on the other hand, she was intrigued to learn more about him as a doctor. What she'd seen so far had certainly been impressive.

She made her way to the clinic and introduced herself to the sister there.

'Could you do a booking visit?' Janet handed her a pile of notes and leaflets. 'First baby, she's down the end on the left. Karen King.'

The booking visit was the first time that the pregnant woman attended the hospital and it took longer than other appointments.

As Tia walked briskly along to the room she found herself looking for Luca and gave herself a firm telling-off.

Why, oh, why did he have such a powerful effect on her?

Pushing thoughts of him from her mind, she opened the door and smiled at the woman seated by the desk.

'Hello, Karen, I'm Tia.' She shook the other woman's hand and settled herself comfortably at the desk. 'This is your first trip to the hospital and this visit does take longer the others. I'm afraid I'm going to bombard you with questions.'

'I don't mind at all.' The other woman's eyes sparkled and she placed a protective hand on her abdomen. 'I've been longing for this appointment. You really feel you're pregnant once you've been to the hospital, don't you think?'

Her excitement and enthusiasm made Tia's heart twist. *Why didn't she feel the same way?*

'Then I gather you're pleased about the pregnancy,' she said, her voice slightly gruff as she opened the notes and pulled a pen out of her pocket.

'I've never been so pleased about anything in my whole life,' Karen said softly, her eyes shining with tears. 'I just can't believe we're going to have a baby. Nigel and I can't stop hugging each other. We've been trying for almost a year. I was really starting to think I wouldn't be able to have my own child and that's a terrible feeling for a woman, isn't it?'

Was it?

Tia stared at her. 'Well, I—'

'All your life you just assume you're going to have children,' Karen continued, 'and then you get married and you assume that you can choose to have a baby when you like, so you try and then nothing happens and it's as if your whole life is over. Do you know what I mean?'

No.

Tia swallowed hard. She didn't have a clue what the other woman meant. Her situation was the complete opposite to Karen's. All of her life she'd assumed that she wouldn't have children. That she would never want to have children. Then she'd become pregnant without even intending to...

'Well, I'm pleased you're pleased,' Tia said quickly, trying to move the consultation away from the emotional side. It was making her feel odd inside.

'How have you been?'

'Pretty sick,' Karen confessed, 'but I read somewhere that if you're sick it means that your hormone levels are high and you're less likely to miscarry. If I lost this baby I don't know what I'd do.'

She looked at Tia anxiously and Tia gave her a reassuring smile. 'You're fourteen weeks now, Karen, and you had a normal scan at twelve weeks. It's unusual to miscarry at this stage.'

Karen gave a shaky smile. 'I hope you're right.'

Tia checked Karen's menstrual history and estimated the date of delivery and asked questions about her obstetric history.

'This is your first pregnancy?' She scribbled in the notes as Karen chatted away, asking questions about Karen's general health and her family history.

'We're all very healthy,' Karen said.

Tia stood up. 'Great. OK, I need to do some tests. Weight, height, test your urine and take some blood. All very routine.'

When she'd finished the tests she sat down and discussed the options with Karen. 'What most people opt for is shared care,' she explained, 'so you visit your GP and community midwife for most antenatal checks and just come to the hospital for key visits. Then obviously you come here to be delivered.'

Karen nodded. 'I definitely want to have this baby in hospital. It's so precious, I wouldn't dream of having it anywhere else.'

She placed a protective hand on her abdomen again and Tia looked away quickly.

Why couldn't she feel like this woman? The truth was,

NO POSTAGE
NECESSARY
IF MAILED
IN THE
UNITED STATES

BUSINESS REPLY MAIL
FIRST-CLASS MAIL   PERMIT NO. 717-003   BUFFALO, NY

POSTAGE WILL BE PAID BY ADDRESSEE

HARLEQUIN READER SERVICE
3010 WALDEN AVE
PO BOX 1867
BUFFALO NY 14240-9952

Get FREE BOOKS and a FREE GIFT when you play the...

LAS VEGAS GAME

Just scratch off the gold box with a coin. Then check below to see the gifts you get!

YES! I have scratched off the gold Box. Please send me my **2 FREE BOOKS** and **gift for which I qualify.** I understand that I am under no obligation to purchase any books as explained on the back of this card.

▼ DETACH AND MAIL CARD TODAY! ▼

306 HDL DUYK   106 HDL DUYZ

FIRST NAME	LAST NAME

ADDRESS

APT.#	CITY

STATE/PROV.	ZIP/POSTAL CODE

(H-P-03/03)

7	7	7	Worth TWO FREE BOOKS plus a BONUS Mystery Gift!
🍒	🍒	🍒	Worth TWO FREE BOOKS!
🔔	🔔	♣	TRY AGAIN!

Visit us online at
www.eHarlequin.com

Offer limited to one per household and not valid to current Harlequin Presents® subscribers. All orders subject to approval.

she spent most of her time pretending that the baby wasn't there—*worrying about Luca.*

But she *was* pregnant.

Panic surged inside her and she stumbled to her feet, suddenly desperate to get away from Karen.

'I just need to arrange for you to see the doctor,' she said quickly as she made for the door. 'I'll be back in a moment.'

Breathing rapidly, her palms damp with sweat, she hurried out of the door and bumped straight into Luca who was walking past.

'Slow down!' His hands shot out and steadied her, his long fingers tightening on her arms as he held her firmly. 'What's happened?'

'Nothing.'

Except that she was having a baby and she didn't have any of the normal feelings.

Luca gave her a searching glance and then guided her into a nearby consulting room which was empty.

'Now, tell me the truth.' He stood with his back to the door, blocking her escape, his dark eyes locking onto hers. 'Something has upset you. What, Tia? Tell me.'

She shook her head, feeling totally foolish. How could she possibly tell him?

He said something in Italian that she didn't understand and closed the distance between her.

'Stop hiding from me.' He cupped her face in his hands and tilted her face up to his. 'You're as white as a sheet and you're shaking. I want to know what has happened.'

Luca's jaw was tense and she sensed that he was angry. With her? For being ridiculous?

'I—It's nothing, Luca,' she said quickly. 'But now you're here, I need you to see a patient in Room 2.' She pulled away from him before his nearness demolished her self-control.

Whatever had possessed her to impose a no-touching

rule? What she really needed now was to feel his arms around her.

'You know something, Tia?' His tone was conversational but his gaze was strangely intense. 'We could be married for a hundred years but we won't ever get to know each other unless you start trusting me with your feelings.'

Tia stared at him.

How? How could she do that? How did she know that he wasn't going to hurt her?

She just couldn't bring herself to take that chance.

'We've got patients waiting,' she croaked, and he gave a wry smile.

'Of course. This is the NHS. There are always patients waiting. We need to talk, Tia, but I agree that this is not a good time.' He stood to one side to let her pass him. 'Who is this lady you want me to see? Is she the reason you're upset?'

Tia walked briskly past him, ignoring his last comment. 'It's a booking visit,' she told him. 'First baby, no problems that I can see. She just needs a routine medical check.'

He followed her out of the room. 'Will you chaperone?'

Tia nodded and took him through to meet Karen.

He talked to her calmly for a few minutes about the baby and then examined Karen's heart and lungs.

'That all sounds perfectly normal,' he said finally, looping the stethoscope around his neck. He finished his examination, scribbled in the notes and then leaned against the desk.

'So…' His voice was warm and caressing. 'Tia has been telling me all about your conversation.'

Tia glanced at Luca with a puzzled frown. What was he talking about? She hadn't mentioned their conversation.

Karen laughed. 'I've bored her to tears,' she admitted with an apologetic smile. 'All I can talk about is this baby and how much I want it. I was absolutely desperate to get pregnant and I can't quite believe it's finally happened.'

Luca gave her a warm smile but his eyes rested on Tia. 'Having a baby is a wonderful thing,' he said quietly, 'although some women have very mixed feelings and that is very natural, of course.'

Tia's heart started to beat more rapidly. Was he addressing his remarks to her? Had he guessed how she felt about being pregnant?

'I don't have mixed feelings,' Karen stated emphatically. 'I'm completely delighted.'

Luca shifted his gaze back to the patient. 'Good.' He gave her a brief smile and stood up. 'You're in excellent health, Karen. You'll be going to your GP next but if you have any problems you know you can phone us.'

With a last smile he left the room, closing the door quietly behind him.

'Oh, that man is totally gorgeous,' Karen drooled as she pulled on her jumper. 'Can you imagine being involved with someone who looks like him? I'd be in a permanent state of faint.'

Tia coloured and Karen gave a gasp and clapped her hand over her mouth.

'Oh, no! You're not…' Her eyes widened and she gave a groan. 'You are, aren't you? And I've just put my foot in it.'

'It doesn't matter,' Tia reassured her quickly. 'And, anyway, you're right. He is gorgeous.'

Karen looked at her dreamily, embarrassment obviously forgotten. 'Does he speak to you in Italian?'

Tia laughed and closed the notes. 'Sometimes. But I don't usually understand a word of it, I'm afraid.' She changed the subject quickly. 'As Dr Zattoni said, your next appointment is with your GP, but you know you can always call us with any problems.'

'Thanks.' Karen stood up and patted her stomach. 'Do you think I'm crazy, being so excited?'

'No.' Tia managed a smile. 'Not crazy.'

100 THE DOCTOR'S RUNAWAY BRIDE

Lucky.

If only her own attitude to pregnancy was so simple.

Tia watched Karen go with mixed emotions, then she worked her way through a steady list of patients and was relieved to stop for a breather when Luca caught up with her later that afternoon.

'Sharon called for you but you were with a patient.' He lowered his voice, aware that people were probably listening. 'She's invited us to supper this evening but I wasn't sure if you'd be too tired. I said I'd call her back.'

'I'd like to go.' Tia stroked her blonde hair behind her ear. 'What about you? You'd like her husband—he's a GP.'

He nodded slowly. 'I met him briefly at the wedding.' He gave a wry smile. 'But I have to admit that I didn't take much notice of him then. I'll tell her yes, but we won't stay late because you look exhausted again and you were so stressed earlier.'

'It's this pregnancy business,' Tia muttered. 'Tiring work.'

He frowned. 'Have you spoken to Dan yet?'

Tia's eyes slid away from his. 'Not yet,' she murmured, purposely vague. 'Give me time.'

'I'll give you time,' he said softly, 'but not too much time. Remember that, Tia. Either book yourself in or I will do it for you.'

Before she had time to accuse him of more male arrogance he turned on his heel and strode away, leaving her staring after him.

With a great effort of will she got on with her work and was forced to call Luca again when she examined a woman who was 32 weeks pregnant and discovered that the baby was breech.

'Does that matter?' Sally Clarke looked at her anxiously and Tia gave her a reassuring smile.

'Not at all, but we do refer breech presentations to the doctor.'

Luca walked into the room at that moment and Tia explained what she'd found.

Sally was starting to look anxious. 'I really don't want to have a Caesarean section,' she admitted. 'It's the one thing I dread. Will I have to?'

Luca shook his head. 'Not necessarily. We will need to keep close eyes on you but a vaginal delivery is sometimes possible. It depends on a number of factors.'

Sally bit her lip. 'Can you turn him around?'

'Not at 32 weeks,' Luca told her. 'He would just turn around again. But that may be an option in a few weeks' time. We'll keep an eye on you and maybe try turning him nearer the time of delivery.'

Luca ordered a number of tests and examined Sally himself.

'I really hurt under my ribs,' Sally grumbled, rubbing herself gently, and Tia smiled sympathetically.

'That's because his head is pressing on your diaphragm.'

She and Luca spent a long time with Sally and Tia made a mental note to try and be on duty when she delivered. She knew that many obstetricians sectioned breech presentations routinely, but clearly Luca was willing to consider letting her try for a normal delivery.

Her shift over, Tia decided to nip up to Special Care to see how little Harry Gibbs was doing. Everyone on the unit was keeping tabs on Sue's progress and were thrilled to hear that she was stable.

Harry was still in an incubator and Eddie was sitting in a chair next to him, reading out loud from a children's book.

'How's he doing, Eddie?' Tia peered into the incubator and Eddie closed the book with a sigh.

'Well, they tell me I've been lucky. Apparently he could have had all sorts of breathing problems, but he seems fine apart from the fact that his sats keep dropping. Whatever that means.' He gave her a rueful look. 'I've been swamped with so many medical terms in the last twenty-four hours that I've given up asking for translations.'

Tia smiled. 'If they're telling you that his sats are dropping, they mean that his oxygen saturation is a little low at times, which is why they're giving him the oxygen. But clearly he's doing brilliantly. Have you talked to Sue?'

'She's still unconscious,' he told her, 'but I sat by her all night. I talked about the baby. Said all the things we would have said together had we known she was pregnant.'

Tia slipped an arm around his shoulders. 'This has been such a shock, hasn't it? And you're coping so well.'

'I don't feel as though I am.' Eddie stared at his son. 'Do you realise, we haven't even got a cot at home?'

'Well, he won't be ready to go home for a while, so don't worry about that,' Tia advised. 'Just get through the next few days. You've got plenty of time to think about the detail. When did you last sleep?'

He looked at her blankly. 'I've no idea. Two days ago?'

'Why don't you go home?'

Eddie shook his head. 'No way. Not until I know Sue's going to be all right.'

Tia racked her brains. 'Wait here.'

She found one of the SCBU nurses and explained the problem. 'Is your parents' room free?'

They had a room available for parents with severely sick children.

The nurse frowned. 'It's free, but if we have a very ill baby—'

'Then Eddie will have to move out,' Tia agreed. 'But at the moment it's the only chance the guy has to get some sleep. Please?'

The nurse nodded. 'I'll clear it with Sister. Tell him to help himself.'

'Thanks.'

Tia gave the news to Eddie and helped him settle himself in the small but adequate bedroom.

Then she glanced at her watch and realised that Luca was probably waiting for her downstairs. And they were going to Sharon's.

CHAPTER SIX

THE minute they arrived at Sharon's, Tia knew it was going
to be a difficult evening.

Sharon was obviously dying for an update and barely
waited until Luca was out of earshot before asking, 'Well?'

'Well, what?' Tia shrugged out of her coat and hung it
in the hallway, one eye on Luca as he strolled through to
the sitting room with Richard, Sharon's husband.

Sexual awareness poured through her veins as she
watched Luca sit down on the sofa, stretching long, muscular legs out in front of him with the easy confidence of
someone totally at ease with themselves.

He was on call and had dressed smartly in well-cut trousers and a black polo-neck jumper that accentuated his
Latin looks.

'He's stunning,' Sharon muttered, following her gaze,
and Tia pulled herself together, wishing she was better at
hiding her feelings.

'Looks aren t important, Shaz.'

And she was fast discovering that there was more to
Luca Zattoni than just looks. She'd learned more about him
in the past few days than in all the weeks that she'd lived
with him in Italy.

'I want to hear everything.' Sharon glanced after the men
and then gestured towards the kitchen. 'Come and help me
in here. We can talk in peace.'

Tia followed dutifully, her eyes flickering over the various pans boiling on the cooker.

'Can I do something?'

'Yes.' Sharon whipped a pan off the stove and placed it

on a mat. 'You can give me an update on your love life. The suspense is killing me.'

Tia shrugged. 'There's nothing to tell. We're fine.'

'Fine? What's that supposed to mean?' Her friend bustled around the kitchen, warming plates and draining vegetables. 'I've been worrying myself to death all week and all you can say is that you're fine? Elaborate! Are you talking? Are you sleeping together?'

'Shaz!' Tia glanced at the door and prayed that Luca wouldn't appear. She'd die of embarrassment! 'Of course we're not sleeping together. We're getting to know each other, remember?'

Sharon stared at her. 'And he was OK with that?'

'Yes, of course.' Tia smiled brightly, trying not to think about the level of tension that was steadily building between her and Luca. It was anyone's guess which one of them was going to explode first.

Sharon lifted a casserole dish out of the oven, obviously unsure what to say. 'And are you getting to know each other better?'

Tia shifted in her seat. 'Shaz, it's only been a few days.'

'But you weren't sure how you felt about him as a person.' Sharon popped a spoon in the casserole and tasted it. 'Do you like him?'

Did she like him?

Tia thought of the times he'd held her when she'd been sick, of the omelette he'd made and the way he'd slept in the spare room even though he must have been hideously uncomfortable. She remembered the candles and the shopping and the warmth he showed to patients and his obvious skill at practising medicine.

'Yes,' she said finally, her tongue licking her dry lips. 'Yes, I like him.'

'And has he mentioned Luisa?'

'No.'

It was the one black spot. He still hadn't been completely honest with her.

'Need any help, Shaz?' Richard stuck his head round the door and looked at his wife. 'We're starving to death out here.'

'Don't rush me.' Sharon shot him a reproving look. 'You can carry the plates through if you want to help.'

The meal was superb and Luca gave Sharon a warm smile. 'This is excellent,' he said quietly, a smile playing around his mouth as he complimented her. 'Truly excellent.'

'Oh. Well…thank you.' Sharon blushed, flustered by the attention, and Tia watched Luca, her eyes resting on his jaw and then sliding down to his broad shoulders.

The need to touch him—to be touched—was becoming an overwhelming ache. She wanted to slip his shirt over the smooth skin of his shoulders and bury her face in his warmth and strength.

His gaze intercepted hers and she knew that he'd read her thoughts. Her heart thumping, she tried to drag some air into her starving lungs, heat flooding her body as she saw the raw desire flare in his eyes.

Sharon's voice broke the spell. 'So are you still being sick, Tia?'

Tia blinked and dragged her gaze away from Luca's, aware of Richard's mild protest.

'Darling, we're eating,' he pointed out, his tone amused as he looked at his wife. 'And you never ask a pregnant person if they feel sick. It instantly makes them feel sick. You're a midwife. You should know better.'

Sharon looked apologetic. 'Sorry.'

Luca smiled. 'Tia is coping very well with the sickness. She is being very brave about the whole thing…' He paused slightly. 'Especially considering how frightened she is about having this baby.'

Tia's face lost its colour and her eyes flew to his. He'd guessed that she was frightened? How?

'She told you?' Sharon gave a smile of relief, oblivious to the tension simmering between her guests. 'Thank goodness for that. I told her you'd understand but she was completely convinced that, being Italian, you wouldn't want a woman who was scared of marriage and children. She has a serious commitment phobia does our Tia.'

Thank you, Sharon.

Tia closed her eyes and wished herself somewhere else. Now that Sharon had confirmed Luca's suspicions, what was there that she could say?

The conversation moved on but Tia was aware only of Luca's dark eyes resting on her from time to time and she knew that the subject was far from closed.

'So what's it like, practising medicine in the UK compared to Italy?' Richard topped up the wineglasses and the conversation shifted to more general topics.

While Luca and Richard debated the merits of various health systems, Tia moved the food round her plate, trying to work out what to say when Luca confronted her in private.

They were finishing coffee when Luca's bleeper sounded.

He pulled a face and went to use the phone, returning minutes later with an apologetic expression on his handsome face.

'They are concerned about a twin delivery,' he explained, reaching for his jacket and car keys. 'I have to go, I'm afraid. Sharon, thank you for a lovely evening. Tia?'

Tia stood up without argument, seeing a means of escape. If she left now, she'd be in bed asleep by the time he arrived home. *Which meant that they could postpone the conversation she was dreading.*

* * *

Several hours later Tia heard the sound of Luca's key in the door. She hadn't slept. Not even for a minute. Her mind was too full of what had happened at Sharon's.

And now Luca was home.

And ready to talk, no doubt.

Hearing his footsteps on the stairs she kept her eyes closed and tried to breathe steadily, knowing instinctively that he would come into her room.

The door opened and there was a long pause. Then she heard him walk across the room and the bed dipped as he sat down.

'Your parents may have been actors, *cara mia*, but they didn't pass on their talents to you,' he drawled softly, stretching out a hand and flicking on her bedside lamp. 'Has anyone ever told you that you are the master of avoidance?'

Tia burrowed deeper under the covers. 'I'm not avoiding anything,' she mumbled. 'I'm just trying to sleep.'

'Don't lie to me, Tia. You have been wide awake all evening, worrying about this conversation,' Luca said, his voice low and rough. 'I saw the expression on your face at dinner. You were horrified that I'd guessed how you felt. Horrified that I have managed to uncover a little part of what you are feeling. You are constantly hiding from me, Tia. Especially about this pregnancy. I need you to be honest with me.'

But was he being honest with her?

She lay still for a minute, feeling a lump building in her throat. 'All right.' She sat up suddenly, her fingers clutching the duvet tightly against her as if she was using it as a barrier between her and him. 'You want to know what I think of this pregnancy? Well, you're right. I am frightened. Actually, I'm terrified. I swore I would never get married and have children and suddenly—' She broke off, her breathing rapid, and wrapped her arms around her knees in a gesture of self-protection. 'I don't expect you to understand. I know that I'm nothing like any woman you've ever met before.'

'Well, that's certainly true.' He stroked her face with a gentle hand. 'But it's not true to say that I don't understand. I want to know exactly how you feel, Tia, and this time I don't want you to hold anything back. You say that you never wanted to get married and have children. Presumably because of your own childhood, no?'

Tia stared at him with dull eyes. She might as well tell him at least part of the story.

'As I told you the other night, my parents' marriage was a disaster,' she said flatly. 'My father had one affair after another—he seemed unable to commit to one woman. And then when Mum died I was passed around a string of foster-homes.'

Luca stroked a hand down her cheek. 'Did anyone try and arrange for you to be adopted?'

Tia gave a sad smile. 'Gawky, eight-year-old bereaved girls aren't that appealing. Everyone wants cute babies. And on top of that I had severe asthma as a child—no one wanted a child with an illness.'

He grimaced. 'So you ended up in a children's home.'

She nodded slowly. 'In the course of my childhood I met children who were the products of bad relationships, children who'd been abused and abandoned. Children who had no one to love them. It seemed to me that being a parent was an enormous responsibility. Probably the biggest responsibility that there is. I swore that I'd never do it.'

But she had. She was pregnant. Panic flooded her veins and her eyes flew to his.

Luca slipped his long fingers through hers and tightened his grip. 'It is true that being a parent is an enormous responsibility,' he said calmly, 'but most families manage to do an excellent job. Your past has given you a distorted view of the truth. Very few children end up in the position that you were in.'

'But for the ones who do…' Tia shook her head and her eyes filled. 'Do you have any idea what it's like? Knowing that no one wants you? It's the loneliest feeling in the world.'

Her voice was little more than a whisper and Luca muttered something under his breath and let go of her hand.

'You are not your parents, Tia.' His voice was gentle as he scooped her up and lifted her onto his lap. 'You are nothing like your parents. You will be a wonderful mother.'

'But what if I'm not?' She stared at him with wide, frightened eyes. 'What if the baby is born and I don't love it?'

Having voiced her biggest fear, she closed her eyes and held her breath, waiting for his horrified reaction.

Instead, she felt his arms tighten around her. 'Is that what is worrying you? That you won't love it? That is a very common fear, you know that.' His voice was deep and very male as he soothed her. 'And some women don't love their babies immediately. I have known plenty of mothers say that they didn't instantly love their babies. For some people it is there straight away, but for others…' He gave a shrug. 'For others love must grow.'

Tia stared at him. 'Do you believe that?'

He nodded slowly. 'I know that you will love our baby.'

She swallowed. 'And what if I don't?'

Would he reject her?

He gave a half-smile. 'You will probably thump me for saying this, but you are very hormonal, *cara mia*, and you are expressing fears that most pregnant women feel at some time.'

Tia shook her head. 'That's not true. That woman in clinic today. Karen. She was so excited about it she made me feel ill. I don't feel like that, Luca. When I think about the baby I just feel panic.'

He said something in Italian and then switched to English. '*That* is why you were so upset today. I guessed as much.' His grip on her tightened reassuringly. 'It's early days, Tia. Karen had been planning a family for ages. That isn't what happened with us. Our baby has come before we planned it and the baby isn't real to you yet. Stop worrying and trust me, Tia. Everything will be all right.'

She lifted her face and her eyes met his. The intensity in his gaze made her heart beat steadily against her ribs and he reached out and stroked a hand down her soft cheek.

He was going to kiss her.

She wanted him to kiss her. She wanted him to kiss her so badly.

His mouth hovered only a breath away from hers and she closed her eyes, her lips parting in readiness for his kiss.

Luca…

She waited in an agony of anticipation and then gave a whimper of surprise and disappointment when he lifted her firmly off his lap and tucked her back under the duvet.

'No touching,' he reminded her, his voice deep. 'We are getting to know each other, Tia, and I want that to continue. For the time being, we talk and nothing else.'

Without another word he walked out of her bedroom, closing the door firmly behind him and leaving her breathless with frustration.

How?

How could he have been so close to kissing her and resisted?

She groaned at the unfairness of it all. When she'd made the no-touching rule she'd had no idea that it would be this difficult to carry through…

Tia was working in clinic again the next morning when Luca found her.

His dark hair gleamed under the lights of the antenatal clinic and he looked strikingly handsome.

'I have arranged for you to have a scan,' he told her, coming straight to the point. 'You need to ask for an hour off.'

Tia gaped at him, outraged by his high-handedness. 'And what am I supposed to tell Sharon? We're rushed off our feet.'

'I want you to see our baby,' he said calmly, clearly unfazed by her anger. 'You are pregnant, Tia, and you can't carry on denying it.'

See the baby? What difference would seeing it make?

And was she really denying it?

Maybe she was.

Tia swallowed, her brain suddenly jumbled. Maybe that was exactly what she was doing.

'All right.' She ignored the sudden fluttering of nerves in her stomach. 'What time is the scan?'

'Twelve o'clock,' he said immediately. 'I'll meet you there.'

She nodded and watched him go with mixed feelings. She knew that the hospital policy was to scan women at about twelve weeks, both to estimate gestational age and to detect any signs of foetal abnormality, but somehow she'd managed to avoid thinking about it.

Until now.

Suddenly feeling very nervous, she went looking for Sharon and asked her if she could take her lunch at twelve and then went back to her patients.

Clinic was incredibly busy but she managed to get away at twelve and made her way to meet Luca.

Most routine scanning was carried out by a radiographer trained in all aspects of ultrasound, so Tia was surprised to see Justin Lee, the professor of foetal medicine, waiting with Luca.

She knew that Professor Lee usually only scanned high-risk pregnancies and she looked at Luca with alarm in her eyes.

'I wanted the best, and I saw no reason to hide our relationship,' he told her quietly, and Justin Lee extended a hand and gave her a warm smile.

'We've all been following Luca's work on pre-term delivery with great interest,' he said. 'I read the last paper he had published and it's been a pleasure to meet him in person and even more of a pleasure to discover that his girlfriend is pregnant! I happen to have a free half-hour and Luca wanted me to do your scan. Is that all right with you?'

Tia nodded slowly. She could hardly refuse to be scanned by someone who was reputedly one of the country's leading foetal medicine specialists!

Justin settled himself on a stool next to the machine and Luca stared over his shoulder.

'This is a state-of-the-art machine,' Justin told him, and proceeded to give Luca the low-down of its capabilities, most of which was beyond Tia's comprehension.

She lay tense and unsmiling as Justin started to scan her, her mind suddenly clouded with panic.

What if something was wrong with the baby?

As if sensing her distress, Luca moved from his place by Justin's side and settled himself next to her, taking her hand in his and encouraging her to look at the screen.

'Watch this,' he urged, his deep voice velvety smooth. 'It's magic, Tia. Our baby.'

Our baby.

Reluctantly she glanced at the screen and her gaze was caught and held by what she saw. The image was so clear she gave a little gasp and Luca's grip on her hand tightened.

'That's an arm,' he told her, watching the screen as Justin carried on with the scan, 'and the head, can you see?'

Oh, yes, she could see.

Suddenly Tia felt as though someone was squeezing her heart.

Their baby...

'He's very active,' Justin said with a smile, pressing some buttons to take measurements.

'He?' Tia's voice was little more than a croak and she cleared her throat.

Justin gave her a smile. 'Not necessarily. I confess that I'm horribly sexist and call all babies he at this stage.'

He made some notes and pointed out some other things he thought would interest them. All too soon it was over and Tia was slipping off the couch and fastening her shoes.

She straightened up and for the first time in her pregnancy her hand crept to her stomach. Suddenly the fear went and she felt incredibly protective.

She only half listened while Justin discussed the results of the scan with Luca, her mind almost completely focused on the living being she was nurturing within her body.

'I'll leave you two alone for a few minutes,' Justin said, gathering up the notes and handing something to Tia.

'What's this?'

She stared down at the photograph in her hands and her vision blurred.

'It's your baby,' Justin said quietly, a smile in his voice. 'Congratulations.'

He left the room, closing the door quietly behind him, and Luca took the photograph out of her hands and placed it on the couch.

'Does it seem so frightening now that you've seen him?' His voice was deep and rough and she shook her head slowly.

'No. No, it doesn't.'

He slid his fingers into her blonde hair and tilted her face up to his.

'How did it feel, Tia, seeing our baby for the first time?' His eyes were gentle. Huge tears welled up in her eyes and rolled down her cheeks.

'It was amazing,' she whispered, a smile breaking out on her face. 'I hadn't really thought about the baby as a person until today, but when I saw him wriggling around...'

'It was very moving,' Luca agreed, brushing her tears away with a gentle hand. 'And now maybe it's time to tell the people you work with that you are pregnant. At least then they are less likely to take advantage of your good nature and overwork you.'

Tia nodded. Suddenly, instead of being an overwhelming problem, the baby was something infinitely precious, to be protected.

'I suppose I'd better get back to the clinic.'

'Don't forget to book yourself in with Dan,' Luca reminded her, and she smiled.

'Has anyone ever told you that you're overbearing?'

Luca gave a smouldering smile. 'You,' he murmured in a deep voice. 'Frequently.'

Just looking into his dark eyes made desire curl deep in her stomach and she forced herself to pull away from him and gather up her things.

She savoured the newly powerful feelings that she had for the baby, marvelling at the way they'd erupted from her heart with no warning. How could she have been so frightened of this baby one minute and so excited the next? It was like a miracle and she snuggled the tender feelings around herself like a blanket.

Suddenly all her fears had gone. She knew that she was going to love this baby because she already loved it. She'd fallen in love with it the moment she'd seen it, just as she had with Luca.

Luca…

It had been love at first sight.

The moment she'd seen him she'd known that he was the only man for her.

And now, the more she knew of him the more she loved him.

He'd known that she needed to see the baby. He'd known that once it had become real she would love it, and he'd been right.

And she knew that she was going to be a good mother.

*   *   *

Tia spoke to Sharon the next morning. 'I think it's time I saw a doctor.'

'At last.' Sharon put her hands on her hips and gave a nod of approval. 'Anyone in mind?'

'Luca wants Dan Sutherland.'

'Good choice,' Sharon said approvingly. 'He's the best there is. Not that you have any worries, with Luca hovering in the wings. He's excellent, Tia. He's got marvellous instincts. You should have seen him yesterday with this difficult delivery that we had. I've never seen anyone so skilled using the ventouse.'

Tia felt a flash of pride. Luca was a very skilled doctor, there was no doubt about that.

'I'll talk to the staff in clinic and see if they can arrange for Dan to fit you in right away.' Sharon picked up the phone and punched in the number, still talking to Tia. 'I assume this isn't something you're trying to keep secret any more?'

Tia shook her head, thinking of Justin Lee. 'Luca seems to be pretty open about our relationship…' She told Sharon about the scan and Sharon's eyes widened.

'Justin Lee did it himself? My, my, you were honoured.' She turned her attention back to the phone. 'Janet? It's me.' Quickly she outlined Tia's situation. 'So can Dan fit her in this afternoon?'

Tia waited while Sharon finished the conversation and replaced the receiver.

'No problem.' Sharon smiled at her friend. 'He'll see you at the end of clinic.'

'Thanks,' Tia said, getting to her feet. 'I need to get back down and do some work or poor Janet may not be so accommodating.'

'Don't overdo it,' Sharon said sternly and Tia gave a wry smile.

'You sound like Luca.'

'Do I? Well, he's bound to be over-protective.' Sharon

gave a short laugh. 'Obstetricians make notoriously para-noid fathers. Unless we keep an eye on him he'll probably have you sectioned at 37 weeks just to be on the safe side.'

Tia laughed. She and Luca hadn't actually got round to talking about the delivery yet.

She made her way back down to clinic and got on with her work.

Halfway through the afternoon she saw a woman who was thirteen weeks pregnant and had severe vomiting.

'I feel so awful,' the young woman confessed, her face pale and wan. 'I can't keep anything down and the minute I see someone else with food I'm sick.'

'You poor thing.' Knowing just how ill she'd felt herself, Tia was very sympathetic. 'Could you hop on the scales for me, Mary? I'll weigh you.'

Mary slipped off her shoes and pulled a face as she climbed onto the scales. 'I know I've lost weight,' she mumbled, glancing anxiously at the reading. 'My clothes are all baggy. I haven't even had to buy any maternity clothes.'

'You can step down now.' Tia checked her weight against the last reading and frowned. The weight loss was significant.

'Is it bad?' Mary gave a sigh and sat back down, obvi-ously feeling as ill as she looked. 'You can be honest—as I say, my clothes are falling off me so I'm already prepared for bad news.'

'It's not bad news exactly,' Tia said quickly. 'But we do need to check you over. I'll just fetch a doctor and then we can talk it through in more detail.'

She found Luca about to drink a cup of coffee and he gave a wry smile.

'I thought a coffee-break was too good to be true.' He stood up and lifted an eyebrow. 'What's the problem?'

She briefed him quickly and he followed her back along the corridor to see Mary.

'By the way, I've just been to ITU to see Sue Gibbs.' A look of satisfaction crossed his handsome face as he gave her the news. 'She's definitely on the mend. Her blood pressure is down and she's sitting up and talking. They're planning to take her to visit the baby later.'

Tia's eyes shone with delight. 'That's fantastic!'

Luca nodded, pausing as they reached the clinic. 'She was lucky she came into hospital when she did.'

'She was lucky she had you when she got here,' Tia said gruffly, and Luca gave her a keen look.

'You were the one who got that airway in while she was fitting, Tia.'

'Teamwork,' she said stoutly, and he smiled his agreement.

'Teamwork.'

They walked into the room to see Mary and Luca introduced himself and flicked through the notes. Then he examined her, carefully explaining everything that he was doing.

Halfway through the examination Dr Ford appeared, her eyes immediately locking onto Luca.

'Sorry I'm late for clinic, Dr Zattoni,' she breathed. 'I was watching Dan Sutherland section a lady with twins.'

'No problem.' Luca quickly updated her and then turned back to Mary. 'I know that this isn't what you want to hear, but you must spend a few days in hospital while we sort out this vomiting. We need to try and find a cause and we need to try and stop the sickness.'

'I thought the cause was pregnancy,' Mary muttered, and Luca inclined his head.

'That's true but sometimes there are identifiable causes. I want to run some tests.'

Mary stared at him. 'What for?'

He rested one muscular thigh on the couch and folded his arms across his chest, totally relaxed as he talked to his patient. 'I want to do thyroid function tests—sometimes excessive vomiting can be caused by thyroid or adrenal dysfunction.' He ticked the tests off on his fingers. 'I want to take some blood so that we can judge how much fluid we should be giving you, and I want you to have a scan straight away.'

Mary sighed. 'How long will I be in hospital?'

'Hard to say,' Luca said honestly, his shrug making him seem more Italian than ever. 'Do you have problems at home?'

'Not at home.' Mary pulled a face. 'At work. I'm a lawyer and taking time off for something like this is frowned on. In fact, my whole pregnancy is frowned on, to be honest. It's just a massive inconvenience to them.'

'And to you?' Luca's voice was soft. 'How do you feel about the baby, Mary?'

Mary paused. 'I thought I could have it all,' she admitted at last. 'I was determined to carry on as I always have, working fourteen hour days until the day the baby arrives, but I never imagined that I'd feel so awful.'

Luca was very still. 'And is your job so important to you?'

Mary seemed to think for a minute. 'Well, I always thought it was,' she said slowly, 'but when they're so unsympathetic, it makes you wonder what it's all for.'

'Pregnancy is a very special time,' Luca said quietly. 'You should take care of yourself.'

'Yes.' Mary nodded and gave him a wan smile. 'Perhaps you ought to have a word with my employers.'

'Willingly.' Luca was totally serious and Mary gave a sigh.

'Only joking. I'll have to face the music myself and tell them I need some time off.'

Tia compared Mary's story with Sharon's reaction to her own pregnancy. She was lucky that the people she worked with were so sympathetic and supportive. Obviously it wasn't the case for everyone.

Luca turned to Dr Ford and issued a stream of orders which left Tia's head reeling. 'Call the ward and admit her, please, and then get a line in and take blood for PCV, U and Es, TFTs. Make sure that the nurses know to chart all the losses and send a urine sample so that we can exclude a UTI.'

Dr Ford scribbled frantically on her pad. 'And shall I arrange a scan?'

Luca nodded. 'Please.'

He stood up and smiled at Mary. 'I hope that a good rest might be enough to sort this problem out. I'll pop and see you later tonight but stop worrying about work.'

Tia tried not to look at his broad shoulders or the powerful muscles of his thighs. Maybe if he'd never made love to her it wouldn't be so bad, but knowing just exactly what Luca could make her feel was starting to drive her to distraction. They'd come so close to kissing the night before, and if she hadn't made the silly no-touching rule she knew that they would have ended up in bed.

As far as she was concerned, the no-touching rule could finish at any time.

She was sure of her feelings and touching wasn't going to change them.

She was totally, utterly, crazily in love with Luca.

But he still hadn't told her about his past.

CHAPTER SEVEN

THE weeks leading up to Christmas were busy and Tia barely saw Luca at home. There was a nasty flu bug going round the hospital and consequently they were very short-staffed.

'You look exhausted,' she muttered one morning as she made them both a quick breakfast before they left for the hospital. 'Can't you take today off?'

'Unless I catch flu, there's no chance.' Luca curved a lean brown hand around his coffee-mug and gave a mocking smile. 'Dan's away this morning and I'm covering his theatre list as well as my own workload. Still, tomorrow is Christmas Eve and we have two whole days to ourselves.'

Tia's eyes widened and she shook her head, puzzled. 'But I'm working.'

'Not any more. Sharon and Dan put their heads together and decided that we need Christmas off,' Luca told her with a smile. 'So tomorrow we're going to buy a tree and do some shopping. We're having a proper family Christmas.'

A family Christmas?

Tia looked at him and swallowed hard. Normally she hated Christmas because she was either on her own or working.

'I—I don't usually bother with a tree,' she confessed, and he gave her a slow smile that made her insides churn.

'Well, this year you're bothering. We're buying the biggest tree in the forest.'

Caught up by his enthusiasm, Tia laughed. 'The ceilings are too low.'

He gave a careless shrug. 'So we cut the top off.' He

121

glanced at his watch and rolled his eyes. 'Come on, or we'll be late.'

Tia had to admit that his stamina was awesome. Despite the punishing hours he'd been working, he still looked relaxed and alert. If it had been her, she would have been in a coma!

'I'm looking forward to having two whole days alone with you. I'm sorry I haven't been home much lately.' His dark eyes were watchful and she shifted slightly under his gaze.

'It doesn't matter. I've been pretty tired, to be honest. I'm usually in bed by nine o'clock anyway if the baby stops kicking for long enough to let me sleep.'

He gave a slight smile and his eyes flickered down to her now rounded stomach. 'He is wearing his mama out and he hasn't arrived yet.'

'Yes.' She blushed slightly. Since that night when they'd almost kissed, he hadn't been near her.

They'd continued to talk and share confidences but he'd kept a distance from her and she didn't know what to do about it.

She'd set the rules but she didn't know how to tell him that she didn't want to live by them any more.

No touching.

She must have been mad. She wanted him to touch her so badly it was a physical ache.

Maybe he didn't want her any more.

Tia was spending more and more time on the antenatal ward where they were always desperate for staff. As it was Christmas, they discharged as many patients as they could, but they were still short-staffed which meant they had to close one ward and merge the antenatal patients with the postnatal patients.

'Another brainchild of the powers that be,' Sharon complained, after another argument with the hospital managers. 'Just because it makes sense on paper, it doesn't mean that it works in reality. Don't these people ever think about the emotional side of things? I've got women with high-risk pregnancies forced to be side by side with women who have just had bouncing, healthy babies. Talk about cruel!'

Tia gave a rueful nod. It *was* cruel and she'd seen the yearning in some of the women's eyes as they'd walked past the breastfeeding room.

Mary, the woman they'd admitted from clinic suffering from hyperemesis gravidarum, had spent several weeks in hospital being rehydrated before finally being discharged.

'It's such a wonderful relief to have stopped feeling sick,' she confided in Tia with a wide smile. 'I just hope it doesn't start again.'

'What happened with your job?' Tia helped Mary zip up her holdall and get ready for her husband, who was collecting her. 'Did they give you the time off?'

'With a great deal of complaint,' Mary said, with a sigh. 'I can see now that I'm not going to be able to carry on in with my current job when I have the baby. I thought that I could do both—you know, the nanny and the high-powered career—but it doesn't work, does it? Not if you want to see the child.'

'No, I suppose not.' Tia bit her lip as she looked at Mary, wondering what she was going to do herself. Luca had grudgingly accepted that she would work while she was pregnant but they hadn't discussed what would happen once the baby was born.

'It's funny how you change,' Mary said softly, slipping on her shoes and picking up her coat. 'I used to think that I wouldn't give up my job for anyone, but now I think that I wouldn't give up being with my baby for anyone.'

Tia nodded slowly. 'I suppose you just have to find an employer who is willing to be flexible.'

Mary laughed and smiled as she saw her husband walking onto the ward. 'Yes, well, that certainly isn't my lot! They're about as flexible as an iron rod. Thanks, Tia.

You've been really great this last few weeks. Thank Dr Zattoni for me, too, will you?'

Tia nodded and walked with her to the door. 'Take care now.'

She watched Mary go and then returned to the ward. Her day was incredibly busy and at three o'clock a woman was admitted with premature rupture of membranes.

'I felt this rush of water down my leg,' she told Tia, 'and at first I thought I'd wet myself—so embarrassing—but then I realised that it must be to do with the baby so I rang the labour ward. What happens now?'

Tia gave her a reassuring smile. 'We need to examine you to see what's going on.'

'But it will be a dry birth, won't it?' The woman looked at her with scared eyes and Tia shook her head.

'There's no such thing as a dry birth, Chloe,' she said calmly. 'That's an old wives' tale. Women used to think that if their waters broke early the birth would be dry, but your waters will always break before the baby is born, even if it's a last-minute thing. It doesn't affect your labour in any way. What it can affect is the health of the baby if your waters break a long time before you go into labour.'

Chloe's eyes widened as she struggled into the unflattering hospital gown. 'How?'

'The fluid around the baby is held in place by a membrane and it means that the baby is totally enclosed in a little bag,' Tia explained carefully. 'If your membranes rupture, the baby is theoretically exposed to germs from the outside world. The most important aspect of looking after you is to check that you don't develop an infection.'

She checked the notes and saw that Chloe was thirty-five weeks pregnant, but before she could examine her Luca arrived with Dr Ford and three students in tow.

'Mrs Hunter, I'm Dr Zattoni.' Luca shook Chloe's hand and gave her a warm smile. 'Could you tell me what happened?'

Chloe looked at him anxiously and repeated her story.

'And you have no pain? Nothing that makes you think you could be in labour?'

Chloe shook her head. 'Will you have to deliver the baby?'

'Not necessarily. A pregnancy can sometimes continue for several weeks without problems. Our concern is to ensure that an infection does not develop.'

Chloe nodded. 'Yes, that's what Tia told me.'

Luca's eyes flickered to Tia and she flushed under his warm gaze.

'All the signs are that the baby is well at the moment. We will do some tests right away and then make some decisions on the best way to manage things.'

Chloe looked at him anxiously. 'What sort of tests? Will I have to stay in over Christmas?'

Luca was noncommittal. 'Possibly. I need to examine you internally to take a sterile sample of the liquor—that is the fluid that surrounds the baby,' he explained. 'That will give us an idea of lung maturity—how well your baby will be able to cope if it is born early. Then I want you to have another scan, just to check that everything is still looking good with the baby.' He turned to Tia. 'What's her temperature?'

Tia nodded and gestured to the chart. 'It's normal. Thirty-six point eight. We'll check it four-hourly.'

'Good.' Luca gave a brief nod and then turned to Dr Ford and gave her some instructions, breaking off as his bleeper sounded.

He lifted it out of his pocket and grimaced. 'Labour ward. I'd better go.' He glanced at Chloe with a smile. 'Tia will arrange for you to have a scan and I will be back to examine you shortly.'

But he didn't reappear. Tia was about to bleep him when Phil Warren, one of the registrars from the other obstetric team, arrived on the ward to examine Chloe.

'Sorry about the delay. It's a nightmare on the labour ward,' Phil muttered in an undertone as he scrubbed and prepared to take the specimen. 'A woman has ruptured her uterus. Luca's trapped in Theatre.'

'What?' Tia stared at him in horror and disbelief. Rupture of the uterus was extremely uncommon in the UK. 'Was it a previous Caesarean section scar?'

Phil nodded. 'She'd already been admitted in labour but the doctor didn't spot it. It was Luca who suspected it—he's seen it before apparently. Anyway, he whipped her into Theatre just in time. She had a massive haemorrhage and it was touch and go with the baby.'

Tia stared at him in horror. 'What did Luca do?'

'Luca?' Phil gave a dry laugh. 'You know him. Mr Cool. He got the baby out so fast we didn't see his fingers move. Funny, really. Every other surgeon I know would have been at least a little tense in that situation but not Luca. He doesn't know the meaning of the word panic. The only slightly stressful moment was when he lapsed into Italian and no one had a clue what he was talking about.'

'And is the mother all right?'

Phil nodded. 'I think so. When I left, Luca had stopped the bleeding, but it looked as though he might have to do a hysterectomy.'

'Poor woman,' Tia said softly.

'Yes, but she's lucky that it was Luca,' Phil said. 'That was a tricky piece of surgery and he undoubtedly saved two lives. I don't think I could have done what he did. He's a bit of a hero on the labour ward today!'

Tia felt a glow of pride. The more she saw of him, the more she realised what a skilled obstetrician Luca was.

Later that afternoon she was moved to labour ward to help out and discovered that Sally Clarke, the woman with the breech presentation, had been admitted earlier in the day.

'Luca is still promising to deliver her vaginally,' Sharon

muttered as she went through the notes with Tia. 'If it was anyone but him I'd be protesting madly, but he's adamant and he does seem to know what he's doing. Can you go and assist? If things go wrong we'll need some extra bodies and, anyway, you know her, don't you? She was asking for you earlier.'

Tia hurried to the labour room and pushed open the door.

Sally was lying quietly, holding tightly to her husband's hand as she listened to Luca.

'You have an epidural in place,' Luca told her, 'because I don't want you to push at the wrong time.'

Tia knew that it also meant that he could use forceps if he needed to.

'I'm never, ever having another baby,' Sally wailed, gripping her husband so hard that her knuckles turned white.

He looked at Luca in desperation and Luca gave him a reassuring smile.

'Everything is fine, I promise you.' He examined Sally carefully and then glanced at Dr Ford. 'This is an extended breech —so that the presenting part is the buttocks. It is the most common type of breech presentation and much safer than a footling breech.' He gave Sally a smile. 'Sometimes they come out feet first and that gives us more of a head-ache.'

Sally gave him a wavering smile, her trust in him clear to see. 'What if he gets stuck?'

Luca shook his head. 'He won't get stuck.' He was to-tally sure of himself. 'We know the size of the baby from the scan that you had, and we know the size of your pelvis from the X-rays.'

Dr Ford stepped closer, her arm brushing Luca's. 'Did she have lateral pelvimetry?'

Luca nodded. 'It shows the shape of the sacrum and gives accurate measurements of the anteroposterior diam-eters of the pelvic brim, cavity and outlet.' He looked at

Sally and gave a sexy, lopsided smile. 'This baby will fit, Sally. Trust me.'

He glanced at the CTG machine and placed a hand on Sally's abdomen. 'You have another contraction coming— I want you to push when I say.' His eyes flickered to Tia. 'Can you chase the paediatrician for me, please?'

Tia slipped out of the room and called Switchboard, knowing that the delivery wasn't far away. She knew that lots of obstetricians chose to deliver all breech presentations by Caesarean section because they were afraid of litigation. It was typical of Luca that he'd allowed Sally to have the delivery that she wanted. His experience and instincts had told him that a vaginal delivery should be safe and he wasn't going to let other people's opinions dent his self-confidence.

She spoke quickly to the paediatrician who assured her that he was on his way, and then returned to the room to find that Luca had delivered the baby's buttocks and legs.

Luca gently pulled down a loop of cord. 'It's important to avoid traction on the umbilicus or the cord might tear,' he murmured to Dr Ford, 'but it is also important not to manipulate or stretch the cord because it can cause spasm.'

Dr Ford leaned closer to Luca. 'What happens now?'

'The uterine contractions and the width of the buttocks will bring the shoulders down onto the pelvic floor,' Luca told her, 'and then they'll rotate.'

He glanced up and smiled at Sally. 'You're doing brilliantly. Nearly there.'

Tia watched as he grasped the baby by the iliac crests and tilted it to free the shoulder.

'I need a towel.'

Tia had warmed one in readiness and she handed it to him quickly.

Luca wrapped it around the baby's hips, improving his grip and also helping to keep it warm.

As the anterior shoulder appeared he placed two fingers

over the clavicle and swept them round to release the arm and then grasped the ankles to free the posterior arm.

'Just the head to go, Sally,' Luca said quietly, infinitely patient as he waited, refusing to hurry nature. 'I wait a couple of minutes and the weight of the body will bring the head onto the pelvic floor.'

Dr Ford looked at him with open admiration. 'How will you deliver the head? Will you use forceps?'

'No.' Luca didn't take his eyes off the patient. 'It doesn't really matter how you deliver the head as long as it's slow and controlled. That's the vital thing to remember. Tia, are you ready to clear the airway?'

'Yes.' Tia got ready with the suction and held her breath while he grasped the baby's feet and, with gentle traction, swept them in an arc over Sally's abdomen, allowing the lower half of the baby's head to slip out.

She quickly aspirated the nose and mouth, making sure that the air passages were cleared.

'All right, Sally,' Luca's voice was deep and controlled, 'I want you to take regular breaths while I deliver the rest of the head.'

He took another three minutes to deliver the baby, allowing the slow release of pressures and tensions on the skull before finally placing the bawling child in the arms of his mother.

'You have a beautiful son,' Luca said huskily, a smile playing around his firm mouth. 'Congratulations. And well done. You were very brave.'

Tears spilled down Sally's cheeks and she reached out a hand to Luca. 'Thank you,' she said, the words choked as she battled with tears. 'If it hadn't been for you I know I would have had a section and I would have hated that. You made it special.'

Luca squeezed her hand. 'You're very welcome,' he said quietly, stepping back as the paediatrician moved closer to take the baby.

It was way past the end of her shift but Tia didn't want to leave until the placenta had been delivered and Luca had finished.

She wanted to go home with him.

As they made for the car park Dr Ford caught up with them and put a hand on Luca's arm, her expression warm.

'You were just amazing in there. There's so much I want to ask you. Shall we go for a drink?'

Tia almost gasped at the audacity of the woman but relaxed slightly as she felt Luca's arm slip round her shoulders, pulling her close to him. 'Not tonight—I've finished work and Tia and I are off until Boxing Day. There'll be plenty of time to answer your questions when I'm back.'

A warm glow spread through Tia's veins as his grip tightened. He was making it clear to Dr Ford that a meeting with her would be nothing but professional.

'Fine.' Dr Ford gave a bright smile that barely hid her disappointment and swung her dark hair over her shoulders. 'I'll see you after Christmas, then.'

'Indeed.' Luca took Tia's hand firmly and led her to the car. 'Get in before you collapse. You must be exhausted. You shouldn't have stayed for that breech delivery.'

Tia's expression softened. 'I like Sally and—' She broke off and blushed slightly. 'And I wanted to watch you.'

Mild amusement lit his eyes. 'Was I being tested? Did I pass?'

His lazy drawl made her blood heat and she struggled to keep her breathing steady.

Oh, yes, he'd passed.

'You were great,' she said gruffly. 'Most doctors would have just sectioned her to avoid the risk of litigation. Dr Ford was right. You were amazing.'

He gave a shrug. 'I don't think so. There was no reason why she couldn't deliver normally,' he said. 'She had a good-sized pelvis and the baby wasn't big, she had a normal volume of liquor, no pre-eclampsia and no foetal distress. It was perfectly reasonable to let her deliver on her own.'

'And what about the woman earlier, the ruptured uterus?' Tia turned to look at him. 'Did you have to do a hysterectomy?'

'No.' Luca shook his head and raked a hand through his hair. 'She was lucky. We managed to repair it.'

Lucky.

Lucky to have Luca.

'Luca…' She turned to face him, feeling suddenly impossibly shy. 'Thanks.'

He yanked on the handbrake and frowned at her. 'For what?'

'For not going for a drink with Dr Ford.' She swallowed hard. 'She's very attractive…'

'And why should that make a difference?' He lifted an eyebrow, his expression deadly serious. 'It's you I want, Tia.'

Did he?

Warmth spread through her veins and for the first time she was tempted to believe him. He certainly didn't behave like a man who was in love with another woman.

He gave her a slow smile and turned the key in the ignition. 'Come on, let's go home and get some sleep. We're going to have a busy day tomorrow.'

'How about that one?' Luca pulled the collar of his wool coat up and narrowed his eyes as he looked at the trees.

Tia picked her way over the muddy path and squinted at the price. 'Luca, it's a blue spruce! It costs a fortune.'

Luca shrugged indifferently. 'Do you like it?'

Tia looked at it again and tried to imagine it covered in delicate white lights. 'It's gorgeous, but—'

'Then we have it,' Luca announced arrogantly, looking around for the man who was helping haul the trees to people's cars.

Fifteen minutes later they were bumping down the forest track with the tree half hanging out of the boot of the car.

'I hope we don't meet a policeman,' Tia said, glancing back anxiously to check that the tree was still mostly in the boot. 'Is it going to fit?'

Luca nodded with his usual confidence. 'It will fit.'

It did. In fact, it was perfect, filling their cosy living room with a musky smell of forest and pine needles.

Tia fingered the needles with awe. 'This is a dream tree.'

'No.' He tucked his fingers under her chin and lifted her face to look at him. 'It's not a dream, Tia, it's real. Remember that.'

He bent his head slowly and brushed a kiss against her mouth and then paused, obviously fighting some internal battle.

She held her breath, wanting him to kiss her properly, but he released her suddenly and gave her a tense smile.

'Come on. We haven't started our Christmas shopping yet.'

The town was crowded and they were soon caught up in the excitement of Christmas, smiling at the groups of carol singers gathered on street corners and admiring the decorations in the shop windows.

They stopped at a small café to drink hot chocolate and eat sandwiches, and Tia's face glowed with excitement.

'You know something,' she said, her hands wrapped around her steaming mug of chocolate, 'this feels like someone else's Christmas.'

He sat back in his chair and gave her a puzzled frown. 'Someone else's?'

'Yes.' She broke off, her cheeks flushed, suddenly shy. 'I was always on the outside looking in at Christmas. It's one of those times of year that always seems to be perfect for everyone else. I know that it isn't, of course,' she said quickly, 'but it just seems that way when you're lonely. This is the sort of Christmas that I always envied everyone

else for having. You know, the tree, the lights, sharing it
with someone you—'

Dear God, she'd almost confessed that she loved him!

Luca was suddenly very still and when he finally spoke
his voice was hoarse. 'Someone that you...?'

Tia's heart thumped steadily. 'Enjoy being with,' she
said quickly. 'Someone you enjoy being with.'

His eyes searched hers for a long moment and suddenly
he looked tired. 'Well, this year it isn't someone else's
Christmas, Tia. It's yours and mine.'

As their eyes locked, her heart started to thump.

Suddenly she didn't care about Luisa or whether or not
she'd been part of Luca's life before she herself had met
him. Either way, she was entirely sure that the woman
wasn't a part of his life now.

'Luca...' how could she tell him that she wanted to end
the no-touching rule?

'Are you ready to go home?'

She nodded and wrapped her scarf loosely around her
neck, dipping her head in its soft folds to hide her blush.

Back at the cottage, they lit a fire and decorated the blue
spruce, smiling with satisfaction as they looked at the results of their handiwork.

Tia had found a holly tree at the bottom of the garden
and had decorated the hearth with twists of greenery and
berries.

'This is wonderful.' She smothered a yawn and stretched
herself full length on the sofa, relishing the view of the
tree. It was a fairy-tale Christmas tree, covered in tiny, delicate white lights and a few tasteful silver decorations. And
under it were presents, gaily wrapped and tied with ribbons
of various colours. She knew that Luca had put them there
and she smiled at him gratefully. 'Thank you, Luca.'

'Prego.' A smile touched his eyes and he knelt down
to tend to the fire, throwing on another log and giving it
a prod.

His black jumper pulled across the powerful muscles of his shoulders as he leaned forward and his jeans were tight over his thighs.

Suddenly her throat dried and she swung her legs off the sofa and stood up.

'Luca…'

He put the poker down on the hearth and turned, his eyes darkening as they clashed with hers.

'Luca, I don't think… I— Would you—?' She broke off, blushing furiously but he rose to his feet in a fluid movement and walked slowly towards her.

She waited, breathless, for him to speak, but he didn't. Instead he stopped only inches away from her, his eyes still burning into hers. And then he lowered his head and covered her mouth with his, lifting his hands slowly and stroking his fingers down her cheeks as he kissed her.

His hands slid round the back of her head, angling her face so that he had better access to her mouth, and she felt the tip of his tongue slide between her lips.

Her body started to tremble and she kissed him back, her tongue tangling with his, her hands sliding under the wool of his jumper and settling on the silken smoothness of his hot flesh.

There was surely no one else in the world who could kiss like Luca.

She didn't feel him move, but suddenly she was lying on the soft rug in front of the flickering fire. They were both breathing rapidly and he stared down at her for a long moment, as if unsure about something.

Surely he wasn't going to change his mind? Not now…

'Luca.' She slid her hands further under his jumper, loving the feel of his hard muscles, loving his strength. Impatient to feel more of him, she pushed the soft fabric up his body and he sat back on his heels and dragged the garment over his head, throwing it carelessly onto the floor next to them.

Tia could barely breathe. Impatient for more, she lifted her hands and reached for his zip.

He smiled. A wicked, intimate smile that made her groan in desperation.

'Patience, *cara mia*.' He lowered himself onto her, carefully supporting his weight on his elbows, and this time his kiss was hot and purposeful, and she knew with a shiver of excitement that this was a kiss that was going all the way.

It was like holding a flame to dry timber. Something inside her ignited and the flames spread, licking through her trembling, quivering body

Her hands slid behind his neck, drawing him closer, and her heart thudded uncontrollably as he kissed her with a savage passion.

Somehow the buttons of her dress were undone and he dragged his mouth away from hers, his breathing laboured, his eyes dark with need as he wrenched the dress down her body. Frantic to feel him against her she used her legs to kick it away, her heart pounding as she felt his long, skilled fingers slip inside the elastic of her panties.

It had been so long…

His name on her lips was barely more than a whisper as he touched her intimately, as only he ever had, his fingers working a magic that left her shaking with need.

Impatiently she pushed his trousers down his hips, feeling the comforting weight of his muscular body press down on her as he parted her thighs. She felt his hard hands on her buttocks as he guided her closer to him and then he paused.

He said something in Italian that she didn't understand, hesitating for just long enough to drive her wild with frustration.

'Luca, please…' She lifted her hips towards him and he altered his position, entering her smoothly and slowly, with none of the fierce desperation that had characterised their previous encounters.

But his touch was all the more arousing for its unusual gentleness. Instead of slaking their need with driving force, he took her slowly, introducing her to an eroticism that she'd never known before. Hypnotised by the heat in his eyes, she gazed up at him, the incredible intimacy between them making her breathless. In the past there had been an edge of violence to their love-making, a mutual desperation that had driven them both wild. But this time his movements were slow and deliberate, building the excitement between them to an almost intolerable level.

Still holding his gaze, she slid her hands over his hard buttocks, urging him still closer, and she felt him move deep inside her, filling her and driving her towards completion.

Then he lowered his dark head and his mouth closed over hers again, his tongue touching hers, tasting, seducing until she felt a throbbing need build inside her. As spasms of pleasure convulsed her body she felt him tighten his grip and knew that he'd reached the same pinnacle.

She held him tightly, her eyes squeezed closed as she tried to bring herself back to earth, tried to cope with the turmoil of her emotions.

Despite all her efforts, tears stung her eyelids and slid down her cheeks. He'd made love to her so gently, so possessively, and yet he still hadn't said that he loved her.

Was he still thinking about Luisa?

'I'm sorry. Did I hurt you?' His rough voice teased her sensitised nerve endings and she shivered as he rolled onto his back, taking her with him.

'No.' She leaned her head on his muscular chest, trying to hide her tears, but he slipped a hand under her chin and tilted her face towards him.

'If I didn't hurt you, why are you crying?'

What could she say? *Because I missed you? Because I love you and you don't love me?*

His arms tightened around her and she closed her eyes, revelling in the physical contact that she'd denied herself for so long. It was so good to be near him, to be held by him.

'You've never made love to me like that before,' she said, her cheeks growing pink under his steady gaze.

'Slowly, you mean?' He gave a wry smile. 'You and I were never very good at taking our time, but this time I was worried about the baby.' His gruff statement made her heart twist.

'You're an obstetrician. You should know better than anyone that making love doesn't hurt the baby.' So that was why he'd been so unusually gentle.

'You haven't answered my question.' He lifted a hand and stroked the tears away from her face, his eyes searching. 'I broke the no-touching rule, didn't I? Is that why you're crying? Are you angry with me?'

His unusual self-doubt touched her.

'No.' How could she possibly be angry? She'd wanted him as badly as he'd wanted her.

She just wished that he loved her.

A frown touched his smooth dark brows. 'Tia?'

How could she tell him the truth? That making love had just confirmed what she already knew. That he was the only man in the world she ever wanted to be with.

'I'm fine. Merry Christmas, Luca.'

The frown disappeared and he smiled. 'Merry Christmas.'

She closed her eyes and nestled against his chest, fighting back the tears again. She wasn't going to cry. She was going to enjoy the moment. All right, so Luca didn't love her, but he found her attractive and she was expecting his baby.

That would just have to be enough.

CHAPTER EIGHT

JANUARY was bitterly cold and Tia threw herself into her work and concentrated on preparing herself mentally for the arrival of their baby.

Her relationship with Luca was becoming closer by the day. And as for their love-making... She closed her eyes and felt her heart miss a beat. It was so spectacular that it was hard to believe that he really didn't love her. In fact, sometimes when they were in bed he was so tender with her that she could almost convince herself that he *did*.

Which was ridiculous, of course, she reminded herself firmly, because he'd never once told her that he loved her in all the months they'd been together.

Fortunately the weeks seemed to fly by and she had to be fitted for a larger uniform to accommodate the growing evidence of her pregnancy.

At work things were as busy as ever but Sharon was careful not to give her too heavy a workload.

'If you deliver early it will just be extra work for us,' she teased one morning as they were sharing a coffee on the postnatal ward. 'How are you feeling?'

Tia smoothed a hand over her swollen abdomen. 'Big,' she admitted with a rueful smile. 'Big and clumsy. And what's worrying me is how on earth it's going to come out.'

She hadn't mentioned her fears to anyone but the thought of the labour was beginning to worry her.

But at least she was excited about the baby now. Even though she was a midwife and knew the theory better than most, she still devoured pregnancy magazines and read everything she could get her hands on.

Sharon grinned at her. 'Is Luca anxious?'

'Luca?' Tia looked at her with surprise and then smiled. 'You're joking, aren't you? When have you ever seen Luca anxious about anything?'

'Never. You're right.' Sharon nodded agreement. 'He's the coolest doctor I've ever worked with but, still, you are his wife and obstetricians behave differently with their wives.'

Tia frowned thoughtfully.

Was Luca anxious?

He certainly didn't seem to be. *Unlike her.*

Fortunately for Tia, the postnatal ward was very busy and she didn't really have time to dwell on her own thoughts and fears.

The weeks passed quickly and she was halfway through an early shift in the thirty-third week of her pregnancy when she felt a stabbing pain low in her abdomen.

She gave a soft gasp and stopped dead, clutching the notes that she'd been about to return to the trolley

The pain gripped her fiercely and then vanished, leaving her tense and anxious.

What had caused it?

She rubbed a hand over the curve of her abdomen, trying to be rational. Towards the end of pregnancy it was normal to feel Braxton-Hicks' contractions, mild contractions that made the uterus tighten up and contract in preparation for labour. She knew that sometimes they could be painful.

Was that what she had felt?

Should she call Luca?

Filing the notes carefully back in the trolley, she decided to carry on with her shift and see what happened. It was bound to be nothing. Maybe she'd pulled a muscle lifting something that she shouldn't have done. What else could it be? She had at least another seven weeks to go until the baby was due.

And she really didn't want to bother Luca with it. He'd only insist that she go home to rest and then she'd have to leave Sharon and the others in the lurch.

As it was, she only had one more week at work and she knew that Sharon had been searching for a replacement.

Determined to carry on, she checked her notebook and noticed that she still needed to do a daily examination on Mrs Burn, a thirty-year-old woman who'd had a forceps delivery during the early hours of the morning.

Putting her own problems to the back of her mind, Tia walked through to the four-bedded ward which was on the south side of the hospital. Despite the fact that it was still only March, the sun shone strongly through the window, making the room bright and warm.

'Morning, ladies,' Tia said cheerfully as she walked briskly up to Mrs Burn. She noticed immediately that the woman looked pale and tired. 'I've just come to do your check, Lisa, if this is a good time for you.'

Lisa nodded slowly and tried to struggle into a sitting position.

Tia frowned. 'Are you in a lot of discomfort?'

Lisa nodded, her eyes filling. 'I can't sit on my bottom at all. It's agony. I know I'm being a wimp, but I can't help it.'

'You're not being a wimp,' Tia said immediately, her expression concerned. 'Let me take a good look at you and then we can decide what to do.'

Tia started out by examining Lisa's breasts, checking that they were soft and free from lumps, redness and soreness. 'How's the feeding going?'

'All right,' Lisa mumbled, 'although I can't sit up at all.'

'Has anyone showed you how to feed lying down?' Tia satisfied herself that everything looked healthy and then helped Lisa wriggle down the bed so that she could examine the uterus. 'For a start, it's so much easier at night just to feed the baby while you're still lying down, and if you're sore down below it will help you not to be on your bottom.'

Lisa shook her head. 'They've been so busy up here since I arrived. Someone did help me latch her on the first time but I've been trying not to bother them since then.'

'You don't have to worry about that. It's what we're here for.' Tia frowned as she palpated Lisa's abdomen. She knew that, like most units, they were very stretched, but it made her uncomfortable to hear that Lisa had been reluctant to ask for help.

Satisfied that the uterus was well contracted and not painful, she asked Lisa various questions and then checked her perineum. What she saw made her wince. No wonder the poor woman was in pain. She had developed a severe haematoma of the vulva.

'Lisa, I can see straight away what the problem is,' she said quietly. 'You've developed a blood clot down below. I'm going to call one of the doctors and ask them to take a look at you.'

Lisa's eyes widened with anxiety. 'Won't it just go by itself?'

Tia hesitated. 'It might,' she said finally, 'but I have a feeling that the doctors might want to sort it out for you. I'll just give one of them a call.'

She bleeped Luca and explained what had happened over the phone, breaking off for a few seconds as the stabbing pain hit her again.

'Tia?' Luca's deep voice was sharp and concerned down the phone. 'Are you all right?'

She sucked in a breath and waited for the pain to pass. 'I'm fine,' she told him, changing the subject quickly. 'So will you come and take a look at Lisa Burn for me?'

'I'll be five minutes,' he said shortly, and she suspected that his haste was as much to check on her as the patient.

She was right.

He strode onto the ward in record time, his dark eyes cloudy with concern as he walked towards her.

'She's in Ward 4,' Tia began, but he raised a hand and stopped her in mid-flow.

'I'll see Lisa in a minute. First I want you to tell me what's wrong. And don't say nothing because I know you well enough by now to know when you don't feel right.'

It was true.

From being someone who didn't understand her at all, he now seemed to be able to virtually mind-read.

'I've felt a sharp pain a couple of times, that's all,' she mumbled, and his broad shoulders tensed slightly.

Maybe he was more anxious than he seemed to be.

He asked her some questions and then gave a sigh. 'You're probably right that it's nothing,' he said, his eyes scanning her pale face, 'but I would prefer that you went home.'

Her eyes slid away from his. 'I'm all right at the moment. If it comes back, maybe I will.'

'Tia…' His voice was a low, threatening growl and she looked at him pleadingly.

'Luca, they're so short-staffed here, it would put a terrible strain on them if I went home. I'm not doing anything strenuous and, anyway, this is the best place to be if something is going to happen.'

She didn't voice her fear, but she was terrified of being at home on her own when the baby came. It didn't matter whether Luca loved her or not—when it came to the baby she trusted him implicitly.

'All right.' He relented, stroking her cheek with lean brown fingers. 'But try and rest as much as you can.'

'I promise.' Tia flushed slightly and her breathing quickened under his touch. 'Are you ready to see Lisa now?'

Luca nodded, his eyes clinging to hers for a long, very unsettling moment. Then he seemed to pull himself together.

'All right. Where is she?'

He examined Lisa and immediately agreed with Tia. 'It's a haematoma. We'll observe it for a few hours and see if it contains itself.' He glanced at Lisa. 'I suspect we will need to take you to Theatre and evacuate the clot.'

True to her promise, Tia was careful not to do anything too energetic during the rest of her shift, and when Luca came back onto the ward to check on Lisa for the second time, she was sitting down, talking to one of the mothers who had just come back from Theatre.

She stood up instantly when she saw Luca and together they had another look at Lisa.

'It's spreading,' Luca said immediately, his eyes quietly sympathetic as he looked at Lisa. 'I'm going to pop you down to Theatre, give you a small anaesthetic and get rid of this blood clot.'

'I'll make the arrangements,' Tia said at once, and busied herself doing just that.

Once she'd escorted Lisa down to Theatre it would be time to go home, but she wasn't at all sure that she really wanted to go.

She hadn't felt the pain for a few hours.

But what if it came back and she was on her own?

She lingered on the ward for another hour and then decided that she was being ridiculous. After all, she could hardly stay at the hospital all night, could she?

Gathering her belongings from her locker, she said goodbye to the rest of the staff and made her way to the car park.

Maybe a warm bath would relax her, and after that she could prepare some supper for Luca.

At eight o'clock Tia was pottering around the kitchen in her dressing-gown when the phone rang.

It was Luca, of course, telling her that he'd be late.

She replaced the receiver and looked sadly at the casserole which was bubbling temptingly on the top of the cooker.

Every time she tried to cook him a nice meal he missed it, but there was nothing that could be done. She turned the heat off with a resigned sigh, helped herself to a portion and then dropped the plate with a clatter as a sharp pain ripped through her abdomen.

Doubled over and gasping, she struggled over to the kitchen table and flopped into the nearest chair, trying hard not to panic.

It was the same pain she'd felt periodically earlier in the day, only this time it was a thousand times worse. It was as if someone was using knives on her insides. Surely this degree of pain wasn't normal? She stroked a hand over her stomach, trying to relax herself, talking quietly to the baby. At least she was still feeling plenty of movements and she knew how important that was.

Suddenly she wished desperately that Luca was at home.

Should she phone him? She glanced at her watch, torn between the need for reassurance and guilt at disturbing him. The probability was that she'd be worrying him unnecessarily.

Maybe she'd just see how she felt in half an hour.

He'd promised not to be too late but he'd also mentioned that he had an emergency section to perform so she knew that he wouldn't be home for a few hours at least.

Tia frowned ruefully at the mess on the kitchen floor. What a waste of casserole! She really ought to clean it up but she was afraid that if she moved the pain might come back.

A glance at the clock on the kitchen wall told her that it was only eight-fifteen. Just a quarter of an hour since Luca had called. Which meant that she needed to fill her time with something or she'd go mad.

Gingerly, still with one hand on her stomach, she stood up, waiting for the pain to tear through her again. Fortunately, it didn't. It was still there, lurking menacingly in the background, but instead of stabbing, it seemed to have settled down to a dull sawing that was more bearable.

She walked slowly through to the sitting room and lowered herself carefully onto the sofa, stretching out her legs and breathing steadily. She felt the baby kick against her hand and gave a soft smile. Whatever was happening, it was good to know that he was still all right.

She flicked on the television and became absorbed in a programme on dolphins, settling herself more comfortably on the sofa. Gradually her eyes closed and she drifted off, only dimly aware of the deep voice of the narrator in the background.

She awoke desperate for the bathroom and clumsily manoeuvred herself off the sofa and up the stairs.

The minute she opened the bathroom door she knew she was bleeding and icy rivers of panic trickled down her spine.

Dear God, no Please, not that...

She needed Luca.

Even as she moaned his name she heard his key in the lock and she sagged with relief and called again, this time loud enough to be heard.

She heard the urgent pounding of his feet on the stairs and then he was beside her, his expression grim as he scanned her pale face.

'*Dio*, Tia—you are in pain again?'

She nodded slowly and straightened, trying to catch her breath. 'Yes, but that's not all.' She broke off and gazed up at him, her green eyes deep pools of fear. 'Luca, I'm bleeding.'

He wrenched his coat off and slung it unceremoniously over the bannister and then steered her towards the chair in the bathroom. 'Why didn't you call me?'

She shook her head and bit down on her lower lip, trying not to cry out. 'I fell asleep. Oh, Luca...' Tears of panic and pain welled in her eyes and she looked up at him, desperate for reassurance. 'What's happening?'

'I don't know yet, but I soon will,' he promised her, crouching next to her, his voice strong and reassuring. 'Trust me, *cara*. We need to get you to hospital. It will be safer to examine you properly there. Will you be all right if I just go and call an ambulance?'

'No.' She grasped his arm and shook her head. 'No ambulance. I don't want you to leave me. Can you take me in the car? Please, Luca?'

He spoke rapidly in Italian and raked long fingers through his sleek, dark hair.

'How much are you bleeding?' He was virtually talking to himself as he checked quickly, his mind obviously working through the options. 'It's not too bad at the moment. All right, we'll go in the car. Can you stand up?'

She hesitated and then nodded, sliding to the edge of the seat and standing gingerly, bracing herself as she waited for the pain to tear at her insides again.

He lifted her easily in his arms, ignoring her protest that she was too heavy, and carried her down the stairs and out to the car.

'All right.' He accelerated away smoothly, driving as quickly as he safely could. 'I want you to describe the pain to me again. Where is it? How does it feel?'

'It's here…' Tia winced and rubbed a hand low over her abdomen. 'Quite low down and it comes and goes.'

'Does it feel like labour?' Luca broke off and shook his head impatiently. 'Forgive me, that was a stupid question. You don't know what labour feels like. Try and describe the pain, Tia.'

Tia looked at him helplessly. 'I don't know if I can. Stabbing, quite rhythmic—it feels as though something's wrong.'

Luca stretched out one hand briefly and rested it on the top of her abdomen. 'It doesn't feel as though you're having contractions. Everything will be fine, *cara mia*,' he said softly, 'but we do need to get to the bottom of the pain and I'd rather we did that in the hospital to be on the safe side. When did you last feel the baby move?'

'Just before you arrived.' She gave him a nervous smile. 'He kicked me really hard.'

He nodded and put both hands back on the wheel. 'Good.'

The trip to the hospital took less than half the usual time and in no time at all she was on the labour ward.

'I want to examine your abdomen.' Luca helped her move into the right position and adjusted her clothing to give him access. 'OK, let's see what's going on here…'

His hands moved gently over her abdomen, a frown touching his handsome features as he examined her.

'The consistency of your uterus is normal. Is there any tenderness?'

'No—not really. It hurts but I don't think it's anything you're doing.'

'I want you strapped to a monitor and I want to scan you. Now.' Luca straightened up in a lithe movement and glanced at Tia who was fighting back tears of panic.

Why, oh, why did this have to happen?

If anything happened to the baby…

She closed her eyes and tried to calm herself down. Luca didn't need her to fall apart.

Scanning her tense features, he pulled her into his arms, talking soothingly in Italian before switching to English.

'Calm down. It will be all right.'

She stared up at him, her eyes frightened. 'If I lose the baby, Luca…'

He brushed her cheek with his knuckles. 'You won't lose the baby.'

'What do you think is wrong?' She shifted slightly on the bed, trying to find a comfortable position.

'I suspect you have a mild separation of the placenta,'

he said quietly, walking towards the door. 'We'll have a better idea once we've scanned you.'

Tia felt as though she'd been showered with cold water and her palms suddenly felt sweaty. *A separation of the placenta.* She should know all about that, but suddenly everything she knew seemed to have vanished from her head. All she could think about was that she couldn't bear the thought of losing the baby.

'I'm only thirty-three weeks pregnant, Luca,' she reminded him hoarsely, her words stopping him in his tracks. 'It's too early.'

'The baby is a good size, and you're only a day off thirty-four weeks,' Luca said firmly, turning as Sharon appeared at the doorway. He spoke to her quietly and then turned back to Tia. 'Let's try not to panic until we know what we're dealing with.'

Seconds later Sharon came in again with the relevant machines and Luca gave her a grateful nod.

'I want to scan her and then I want her on a monitor. And could you call Dan Sutherland? I'd like his opinion.'

'Well, he certainly owes you some time after all the clinics and Theatre lists you've covered for him this week,' Sharon said immediately, her eyes on Tia. 'Don't you worry. You're in the right place now and that baby of yours is going to be just fine.'

Tia forced back the tears that were threatening. She hoped they were right.

Luca scanned her carefully, checking the position of the placenta and looking for concealed bleeding.

'There.' He leaned forward and touched the screen with his finger to show Sharon what he'd noticed. 'The placenta is in the upper segment and I can see just a small concealed bleed. I want her kept on a monitor, Sharon.'

Tia licked dry lips. 'My placenta is coming away?'

Luca looked at her hesitantly. 'Yes. But it's only a small area—'

'Luca, I'm a midwife,' she reminded him in a croaky voice. 'Small areas can become big areas.'

He sat down on the bed next to her, taking her hands in his. 'Tia, now that we know what the problem is, we can deal with it. The baby is absolutely fine at the moment. He is still getting plenty of oxygen. We're going to admit you to the ward here and you're going to take it easy for a few days while we watch you.'

A lump grew in her throat at the thought of being on her own in a sterile hospital room.

She wanted to go home to their cottage.

'This is all my fault,' she whispered, placing a protective hand on her abdomen. 'The baby must have known that I didn't want it, but now I do, desperately, and—'

'Hush.' Luca's voice was firm but kind. 'Don't torture yourself. The feelings you had were perfectly normal. They certainly have no bearing on the fact that you're bleeding. You need to try and relax, Tia. Please.'

Tia took a shuddering breath and tried to pull herself together. 'I want to be at home—' She almost said 'with you' but stopped herself just in time. The last thing he wanted was her all over him. They were good friends and they had an amazing sex life, but that was it.

'Well, if you're worried about not seeing Luca, don't be,' Sharon said briskly, helping Tia back into the wheelchair. 'The man has a second home here in case you hadn't noticed. He can sleep in the spare on-call room on the ward if he likes.'

'Good idea.' Luca nodded immediately. 'I'll pick up some stuff later and move in until you're sorted out.'

The knowledge that he'd be close to her made her relax for the first time since she'd arrived at the hospital, and she gave him a grateful smile.

He might not love her but she certainly couldn't fault the way he behaved towards her. He was very attentive and caring.

'Right.' He rubbed a hand over his face and took a deep breath, obviously marshalling his thoughts. 'Let's get you up to the ward and then I want to do a haemoglobin, a coagulation screen and a Kleihauer test.'

Dan Sutherland strolled into the room at that moment, his expression concerned as he looked at Tia.

'What's been happening to you, then?'

Luca filled him in and Dan nodded slowly. 'Right. We really need to do a speculum examination as well. Would you rather I did that?'

Tia nodded, her cheeks flaming red. It shouldn't have been embarrassing to be examined by Luca but she knew that it would be.

Sensitive to her feelings, Luca mentioned something about fetching some blood bottles and strode out of the room, leaving her with Dan and Sharon.

'Poor chap.' Dan glanced after him, a sympathetic expression in his eyes. 'It's never easy, having someone you love as the patient. He looks so stressed.'

Tia was hardly aware of what Dan was doing as he carried out his examination. It was true that Luca was stressed, but she knew that it was because of the baby, not her. She knew just how much the baby meant to him.

'The bleeding is definitely from the uterine cavity,' Dan said finally, tearing off his gloves and tossing them in the bin. 'How far on are you? Thirty-three weeks—nearly thirty-four.' He frowned down at her notes, lost in thought. 'All right. Sharon, let's give her some dexamethasone because I have a feeling that this baby might decide to make an appearance early.'

Tia felt her heart lurch. She really, really didn't want the baby to come early. She wanted to have a normal, healthy full-term baby like everyone else. What had she done to deserve this? Why couldn't she have had the sort of birth that she'd read about in the glossy magazines?

Tears pricked her eyes and she cursed herself for being

so emotional. Before she'd become pregnant she'd considered herself to be a resilient person, someone who hardly ever cried, but today she felt as though there was a dam inside her, waiting to burst.

Sharon must have noticed because she waited for Dan to leave the room and then slipped her arms around Tia.

'You poor thing. You must be so worried, but try not to be, sweetheart. We'll sort you out. Have a good cry if you need to. It's mostly hormones, you know that as well as I do. And disappointment.' She nodded wisely, the gentle expression in her eyes showing that she'd understood everything that Tia was feeling. 'Everyone assumes that they'll have a normal pregnancy and delivery but it doesn't always happen that way.'

Tia sniffed and rubbed away the tears with the back of her hand. 'I don't know why I'm being so pathetic.'

'Because you're worried,' Sharon said simply. 'We all have certain expectations about childbirth and when things deviate from what we're expecting we feel cheated, but the truth is that plenty of people have less than perfect textbook births.'

'I know.' Tia sniffed again and gave a watery smile. 'I just want the baby to be OK.'

'Tia, nothing is going to happen to your baby with both Dan and Luca in charge,' Sharon said soothingly, gathering up Tia's belongings and handing them to her. 'Now then, can you manage these on your lap if I push you in the wheelchair?'

Tia nodded. 'Thanks, Shaz.'

Sharon pushed her up to the ward and helped settle her into a side room.

'I feel guilty, taking a side room,' Tia mumbled, and Sharon waved her hand dismissively.

'Nonsense. It's the least we can do for you and, anyway, for once we're not actually that busy at the moment. If we have to move you out, we will. In the meantime, the room is yours.'

Tia settled herself on the bed and gave a sigh. 'Am I allowed to move around?'

'Well, there's no way I'm bringing you a bedpan, if that's what you're asking,' Sharon said dryly. 'But, seriously, I think you should take advantage of the opportunity to get some rest. How's that pain now?'

'About the same,' Tia admitted, rubbing a hand across her swollen abdomen.

'OK. Well, I'm just going to sort out that dexamethasone and then we need to do those blood tests Luca requested.' Sharon walked towards the door and propped it open, smiling as one of the student midwives entered. 'Have you been shopping?'

'As instructed.' The girl passed two bags to Sharon who walked back into the room armed with magazines, books and flowers. 'Here we are—a few things to keep you occupied.'

Tia started to laugh as she poked through the bags. 'Shaz, I can't possibly eat all that chocolate! I'm the size of a house already.'

Sharon put her hands on her hips and surveyed Tia through narrowed eyes. 'Not a house. More a small cottage, I should say, but it doesn't matter because the chocolate isn't for you. It's for us poor midwives who have to look after you.'

Tia shook her head, still smiling. 'And I suppose you're going to hide in here and read my magazines as well?'

Sharon clicked her fingers. 'Bother. You've rumbled my clever plan.'

'Thanks, Shaz.' Tia folded her legs underneath her and reached for one of the magazines. Maybe being in hospital wouldn't be so bad after all.

At least she felt safe.

CHAPTER NINE

SHARON sorted out the injection and the tests and then suggested that Tia take a nap.

When she awoke it was dark on the ward and Luca was sprawled in a chair by her bed, his eyes closed. Dark stubble was beginning to appear on his hard jaw.

'Luca.' She struggled to sit up, strands of sleek blonde hair falling over her eyes. 'How long have you been here?'

'About an hour and a half.' He suppressed a yawn and gave her a sleepy grin that did something strange to her insides. 'I've had a really good sleep. It seems that while no one seems to give a second thought to bleeping me at home, if I'm in my girlfriend's hospital room I'm given total peace and quiet. I'm thinking of leaving you here permanently.'

She smiled. 'I'm sorry I woke you.' Her voice was still scratchy with sleep and he reached out a lean hand and switched on the bedside lamp so that he could see her more clearly.

'How's that pain?'

Tia considered for a moment, rubbing her hand gently over her precious bump. 'Better,' she said with a nod. 'Definitely better. Maybe rest was all it took.'

'Let's hope so.'

Tia bit her lip, anxious for reassurance. 'Do you think the baby is all right, Luca?'

'The baby is fine,' he murmured, his voice deep in the semi-darkness. 'You are still feeling movements and I saw the trace that you had done before you went to sleep. There is no evidence of foetal distress. Go back to sleep now. The best thing that you can do for that baby is get some rest.'

Rest.

Tia snuggled back down under the covers and did as he'd suggested.

When Tia finally awoke the next morning she was feeling much better.

The pain had all but gone and the prospect of a day doing nothing but lying on the bed, watching television and reading the magazines that Sharon had brought her was suddenly very appealing.

There was no sign of Luca but presumably he'd had to leave before she'd woken up. She knew that he usually did a ward round first thing in the morning.

It was only as she lay doing nothing that she realized just how hard she'd been finding it to be on her feet all day at work.

One of the nurses brought her breakfast and she sat in bed and munched toast and drank tea.

'Lady Muck.' Sharon arrived a few minutes later, a broad grin on her pretty face. 'I'd be feeling quite jealous if it weren't for the fact that I'm about to stab you in the bottom with another injection of dex.'

'Oh, thanks.' Tia pulled a face. She'd forgotten that she was due to have another steroid injection. She knew that they gave steroids to women under thirty-four weeks because they helped to mature the baby's lungs in the event of a premature delivery.

She chatted to Sharon while she finished her toast and then wriggled down on the bed, screwing up her face as Sharon gave her the injection.

'I hope you don't expect me to thank you,' she grumbled, pulling her nightie down and sitting back up. 'Horrible.'

'Yes, well, with any luck it will have been for nothing. If you hang onto that baby, you won't need it.' Sharon sat down on the edge of the bed and checked Tia's pulse and blood pressure.

'Midwives should not sit on the bed,' Tia recited, and Sharon grinned.

'But I'm the boss. Are you going to report me?'

'Not for that. But if you carry on stealing chocolates when I'm asleep then I definitely am.' Tia shook her head, her expression one of complete disbelief as she watched Sharon eat four chocolates in quick succession, even though it was only breakfast-time. 'I've never known anyone eat as much as you. How do you stay so slim?'

'It's probably something to do with running round after people like you.' Sharon stood up and scribbled on the chart. 'Well, that's all fine. You're pretty healthy for someone who looks like a baby elephant.'

Tia laughed. 'I am huge, aren't I?' Then she stroked her bump anxiously. 'The scan didn't indicate I was any bigger than average but I feel like I've swallowed a balloon.'

'I suppose that's because you're basically a very small person,' Sharon observed, her eyes sweeping over Tia's arms and legs. 'Any size of baby would seem massive on you. Any more bleeding or pain, Tia?'

Tia shook her head and they chatted for a while longer, then Sharon went off to do her work and Tia snuggled down and promptly fell asleep again.

Tia woke up in time to eat her lunch and then slept right through until teatime when Luca strolled through the door.

Tia felt her heart miss a beat.

He was a spectacularly good-looking man.

She couldn't take her eyes off him as he sat down in the armchair by her bed and stretched long, powerfully muscled legs out in front of him.

'What a day.' He closed his eyes and let out a long breath. 'No one seemed to be able to manage a normal delivery.'

Safe in the knowledge that he wasn't watching her, Tia treated herself to a long look at him, her eyes sliding over his thick, dark lashes and resting on his roughened jawline.

He was enough to give a woman a heart attack.

His eyes opened and his expression changed as he intercepted her look.

'Tia?' His voice was gruff and he rose to his feet and settled himself on the edge of her bed, a strange light in his eyes. 'How are you feeling? Sharon told me that you've slept for most of the day. That's good.'

His nearness was making her whole body weak and before she could stop herself she reached out a hand and drew his head down to hers.

With a low groan his mouth closed over hers, his tongue seeking entrance as he kissed her slowly and thoroughly.

Her heart thumping, she felt one of his hands slide into her hair, holding her head immobile so that he could increase his access to her mouth.

Her body started to ache and burn as his tongue explored her intimately, his kisses growing deeper and more demanding. His free hand slid gently over her breast, cupping the fullness, teasing the peak with the rough pad of his thumb until she thought she'd go mad with frustration.

By the time he finally lifted his head she was shaking so badly that had she not already been lying on the bed her legs would certainly have given way.

'Cara.' His voice was thick with passion and he brushed his knuckles over her flushed cheeks with a rueful smile. 'I'm sorry. I should have shaved before I kissed you.'

'It doesn't matter.' Her eyes dropped to his dark jaw and desire curled deep inside her.

'Do you realise that is the first time in the whole of our relationship that you have touched me first?' His voice was soft and his eyes were strangely penetrating, as if he was trying to read her mind.

Tia dropped her eyes, thinking to herself that it was a good job that he couldn't read her mind or he'd be able to see just how much she loved him, and she didn't want that.

It would be more than her pride could bear to let him know just how deep her feelings were for him.

There was an exaggerated cough from the doorway and Sharon stood there, a wicked grin on her face.

'Sorry to disturb you two lovebirds. I'm supposed to be checking your blood pressure, Tia, but it's going to be sky high after that!'

Luca laughed and stood up slowly, as relaxed and self-possessed as ever.

'Absolutely. Better give her five minutes to get her breath back.'

Tia watched him curiously, her cheeks still flushed. He didn't seem to mind at all that Sharon had caught them kissing.

Still smiling, Sharon checked Tia's pulse and blood pressure and then listened to the foetal heart.

'You shouldn't be doing all this,' Tia said, watching her friend recording all the results. 'I ought to have a student midwife.'

Sharon looked horrified at the mere suggestion. 'I've already told you—we're not that busy today, so you can have star treatment.'

'Let's put her on the monitor for an hour,' Luca suggested, rubbing a hand over his face and suppressing a yawn. 'I might go and have a shower while you do that.'

He touched his rough jaw and looked at Tia with an apologetic smile.

'You go,' she said softly. 'I'll see you later.'

Luca left the room and Sharon sighed.

'That man is seriously gorgeous, Tia.'

'I know.'

Sharon's eyes narrowed. 'You do realise that he's crazily in love with you, don't you?'

Tia's eyes widened and she shook her head. 'Don't be ridiculous.'

'I'm not being ridiculous,' Sharon said, her tone dry.

'The man is crazy about you. For goodness' sake, Tia, why do you think he can't stay away?'

Tia shrugged. 'He's worried about the baby.'

Sharon arched an eyebrow. 'Oh, right. And wild, passionate kisses are the latest thing for averting pre-term labour, are they?' She gave a grin. 'I must have been reading the wrong research papers.'

Tia flushed. 'You've got it all wrong.'

'No.' Sharon's smile faded and she shook her head. 'It isn't me who's got it wrong, angel, it's you.'

'So if he's crazy about me, why hasn't he told me?' Tia asked, trying to sound indifferent.

Sharon gave a shrug. 'I don't know. I admit that's a mystery. But you haven't exactly been honest with him about your feelings either, have you? When did you last tell him that you love him?'

Tia shook her head. 'Not since that fiasco on the day of the wedding that wasn't.'

'Precisely.' Sharon breathed out heavily and shook her head. 'What a mess. The two of you need to have your heads knocked together.'

Tia bit her lip. 'Sharon…'

'All right, I'll drop it.' Sharon looped her stethoscope around her neck and moved towards the door. 'But take my advice. Any man who can kiss a woman like that is worth hanging onto.'

Tia watched her go with a faint smile. There was no doubt that Luca knew exactly how to kiss a woman senseless.

She touched her mouth with her fingers, remembering just how that kiss had felt.

Incredible.

But she still couldn't bring herself to tell him that she loved him. It would make her too vulnerable.

An hour later Sharon popped her head round the door to

tell her that Luca had been called down to Theatre and had said that Tia should have an early night.

Hiding her disappointment, Tia closed her book and snuggled down in bed, deciding to take his advice. Sleep certainly seemed to be helping. She felt better than she had for ages.

The baby was still very active and the pain had gone.

Maybe there really was nothing to worry about.

Tia awoke when the pain hit her.

With a muted gasp she struggled to sit upright, her hand pressed to her abdomen as the severe cramping pain tore through her insides.

Groaning softly, she bit back a sob and realised that the room was still empty. Luca obviously hadn't come back. Eyes closed, she breathed gently, hoping that the contraction would soon pass. Because that was undoubtedly what it was. She'd never had a baby before so she didn't have first-hand experience of labour pains, but the hand she had placed on her abdomen told her everything she needed to know.

She was definitely in labour.

Six weeks early.

Trying not to panic, she took shallow breaths and waited for the pain to pass. Finally she was able to reach out and press the buzzer.

Polly, the night sister, was by her side in an instant. 'Problems?'

Tia nodded, her lower lip caught between her teeth. 'I'm in labour, Polly. Or at least I think I am.'

'Can I have a feel?' Polly sat down on the bed next to her and placed a hand on Tia's bump.

Tia tensed as another pain hit and Polly glanced at her watch, timing the contraction. After a few minutes she stood up and bustled around the room.

'I'm going to put you on a monitor,' she told Tia, 'but

it does look as though you're in labour. I'll call Dan Sutherland.'

'Where's Luca?' Suddenly Tia desperately wanted him to be with her. It didn't matter whether he loved her or not. She trusted his judgement and she felt safe with him.

'He was in here having a kip and then he was called down to labour ward again,' Polly told her. 'One of the registrars was having problems with someone and popped up to ask his opinion.'

And she hadn't even heard him leave. She must have slept like the dead. 'Will you call him for me?'

Polly nodded. 'Right away.'

Tia watched her leave the room and tried not to panic. The baby should be fine. She was just thirty-four weeks pregnant, which was early, of course, but not as seriously early as it might have been. The baby might well have problems, but surely he shouldn't die?

Polly was back in the room a moment later with the CTG machine. The CTG—or cardiotocograph—gave a graphic record of the response of the foetal heart to uterine activity, as well as information about its rhythm and rate.

Tia shifted in the bed until she was more comfortable and then Polly strapped an ultrasound transducer to her abdomen.

'Right...' Polly adjusted the strap and fiddled with the machine. 'Let's see what this tells us...'

Tia relaxed slightly as she heard the reassuring galloping of the baby's heart.

Polly's eyes were fixed on the machine and she rested a hand on the top of Tia's abdomen to feel for any contractions.

Seconds later Tia felt the pain begin to build and grip her. With a moan she shifted again, trying to find some relief from the agony, but the pain was so intense she could barely breathe.

'Well, you're definitely having strong contractions,'

Polly muttered, watching the machine and then glancing at Tia. 'I'll go and try Luca again.'

'I'm here.' His deep voice came from the doorway and he entered the room, his handsome face strained as he instantly assessed the situation. 'You are in labour, *cara*?'

The concern on his face and his gentle endearment made her heart turn over.

'I think so.' She nodded and gasped as another pain tore through her. 'Oh. Luca…'

He was beside her in an instant, sliding a lean, brown hand over her abdomen, feeling the strength of her contraction, murmuring encouragement to her as she tried to remember how she was supposed to breathe.

She sagged against the pillows as the contraction ended. 'Can we stop the labour? I don't want it to come early.'

Luca squeezed her hand and got to his feet in a fluid movement and looked at the trace on the CTG machine. 'We need to examine you.' He turned to Polly. 'Have you called Dan?'

'Yes.' She nodded confirmation and Luca's mouth tightened.

'Well, call him again,' he growled, moving back to Tia, his tension obvious.

Polly vanished and reappeared a moment later with Dan, who was the epitome of calm efficiency.

'You're determined to have this baby early aren't you?' he said lightly, smiling at Tia and taking the trace Luca handed him.

The next half-hour was a whirl of tests and discussions, and all the time Tia struggled to cope with the contractions, which were becoming more powerful by the minute.

Finally Luca raked a hand through his hair and sat down on the edge of the bed.

'We have all talked about it and we are agreed that we need to get this baby out, Tia,' he said quietly, his dark eyes holding hers. 'I know you don't want to have it early, but we don't have any choice. Your labour is too advanced to stop it, and there is some evidence of mild foetal distress.'

Tia's eyes widened anxiously. 'How mild?'

'Our baby is fine at the moment,' Luca reassured her quickly, 'but we are all agreed that we should deliver him or her as soon as possible. How do you feel about having a section?'

Tia swallowed. This wasn't happening the way she'd expected. Naïvely she'd expected a perfectly normal delivery—the sort that she'd helped so many women with since she'd qualified as a midwife. She'd never thought that she'd be in the 'complications' category.

Suddenly she felt hideously frightened and it must have shown because Luca quickly turned to his colleagues.

'Give us five minutes alone, please.'

They obeyed immediately and Luca moved closer to Tia and took her hands in his.

'What is it that you're afraid of?'

She shook her head, unable to articulate her feelings. 'I don't know—everything. I'm afraid of the baby coming early, I'm afraid of having surgery.' Her heart thudded faster and she looked at him with scared eyes. 'I didn't want it to be like this. I thought it would all be normal.'

His grip on her hands tightened. 'Not everyone is given the perfect delivery,' he said softly, 'but what matters in the end is that you are both fine. The rest of it we can deal with. Dan is one of the best surgeons I've ever seen and I'll be there the whole time—'

'Can't you do it?'

His jaw tensed and for the first time in her pregnancy she thought she detected signs of strain in his face. Maybe he wasn't quite as relaxed as he liked to pretend.

'Tia, you know I wouldn't be the best person for this.' His eyes locked with hers and he smoothed her hair away from her face. 'I cannot operate on the woman I— on my girlfriend,' he amended quickly. 'Dan is the best person.'

'Can't I have a normal delivery?'

Luca let out a long breath. 'We could start that way and see how it goes, but you're bleeding again and I'd rather we were in control of the situation from the start. My instincts are that we should get the baby out now.'

And he had the best instincts of any doctor she had ever met.

'All right.' Tia pulled herself together and gave a nod. 'I just want the baby to be safe. Let's get on with it, then.'

'We'll give you an epidural,' Luca said, standing up and making for the door. 'I'll bleep the anaesthetist.'

The thought of having an epidural frightened her as well, but she knew that it was much safer for the baby than a general anaesthetic. But what would it be like to be awake as the baby was delivered?

She tried to be rational. At least if she had an epidural then she'd be able to be a part of the birth.

And Luca would be there.

Fighting down the panic, Tia gave Luca a smile, but she knew from the growing concern in Luca's eyes that he understood exactly how she was feeling.

'We'll give you some gas and air until the anaesthetist arrives,' Polly said briskly, pulling the machine closer to the bed. 'Do you want me to remind you how to use it?'

Tia gave a weak smile. They were all shown how to use it in their training, of course, and she helped women use gas and air on an almost daily basis, but it was quite a different matter to be the patient!

'I tried it once when I was training,' she told Polly. 'It made me feel dizzy.'

'Yes, well, dizzy might be a pleasant change from the pain,' Polly observed, her gaze sympathetic as Tia gave another groan as a contraction gripped her. 'Let's give this a try, and don't breathe too quickly. That's usually why people get dizzy, as you know.'

Polly handed her the mouthpiece and Tia breathed steadily, screwing up her face as the pain intensified.

'Well done. Good girl.' Polly encouraged her gently through the contraction and Luca slid an arm round her shoulders, hugging her against him as the contraction ended.

'You need to start using the gas and air as soon as your uterus starts to harden,' Polly reminded her, and Tia nodded, her face pale and drawn.

Luca stroked her hair and softly spoke to her in Italian.

'What?' Tia looked at him, pain making her uncharacteristically grumpy. 'What did you say? I didn't understand you.'

Something flickered in his dark eyes and he hesitated. 'I said that it will soon be over,' he muttered, and Dan shot him a strange look.

'What? But I thought—' He broke off as he caught Luca's eye. 'Well, I mean…my Italian never was any good, anyway.' He cleared his throat and turned his attention back to the notes just as Duncan Fraser, the anaesthetist, hurried into the room.

'I'm such a wimp,' she gasped, clutching Luca and pushing away the gas and air. 'Why do women ever want natural births?'

She'd never known such agony.

'Labour is never the same for two people,' Polly reminded her gently, rubbing her back to try and help relax her. 'I've seen women deliver in hours and barely notice, and so have you. It isn't a competition, Tia. You just have to do what's right for you.'

Duncan made the necessary preparations and then moved closer to the bed. 'When this contraction has passed I need you to sit on the edge of the bed for me. We're going to need to work in between contractions, Tia, so if you feel another one coming, warn me.'

Tia did as he instructed, gripping Luca's hand tightly.

'All right, Tia.' Duncan explained what he was doing in a calm voice and in no time at all the epidural was in place and the awful pain was fading to nothing.

'Does that feel better?' Luca's eyes were clouded with concern and she nodded.

'Much.'

'We're going to take you through to Theatre now, Tia.' Dan issued some instructions and Tia closed her eyes as they wheeled her through the swing doors.

Why had this happened to her? Here she was, about to be operated on while she was awake. The thought terrified her!

Sensing her anxiety, Luca spoke quietly to Dan and then settled himself on a stool by Tia's head and took her hand firmly in his.

'It's time we thought of some names,' he said, his eyes warm as he held hers. 'Something Italian, of course—Luigi, Leonardo, Gianfranco…'

Despite her nerves Tia smiled, grateful that he was trying to distract her. 'What if it's a girl?'

He gave a sexy grin. 'I hope it is. I'm better with women.'

And didn't she just know it!

Ignoring the flash of disquiet that his comment caused, Tia concentrated on thinking of girls' names, only dimly aware that Dan had started operating. 'Daisy?'

'Daisy?' Luca gave her a horrified look. 'What sort of a name is Daisy? Is that the best you can come up with?'

'I think it's pretty,' Tia muttered, her eyes rested on Luca's thick, dark lashes and the hard angle of his cheekbones. 'Or how about Lily?'

'What is this preoccupation with flowers?' For a brief

second Luca's gaze flickered over the green sterile towels to his colleague who gave him a reassuring nod.

'I like Lily,' Tia said huskily, starting to relax now that she realised she really couldn't feel anything.

'You are feeling all right?' Luca's voice was gruff and she gave a slow nod.

'Yes, surprisingly enough. I can just feel some pulling, but it doesn't hurt.'

'I should think not!' Duncan looked horrified at the mere suggestion that any anaesthetic he administered could be less than perfect. 'How are you doing there, Dan? Any time in the next ten hours is fine by me.'

Despite the banter, Tia knew that Dan was working quickly and only seconds later there was a slight commotion and Luca straightened up, his features tense as Dan lifted the baby out.

'Looks like you've got your flower, Tia,' Dan said cheerfully as he handed the baby to Luca. 'It's a little girl.'

'Oh!' Tia stared, wide-eyed, as Luca held the bawling bundle close to her. 'Oh, Luca...'

Tears slipped down her cheeks and she looked at the baby in amazement, thinking that she'd never seen anything so beautiful in her life.

'Can we call her Lily? Please?' Her voice was choked and for a moment Luca didn't speak, his dark eyes unusually bright as he held his tiny daughter in his hands.

'Lily sounds good to me,' he said finally, his voice decidedly rough around the edges. 'Lily Zattoni.'

CHAPTER TEN

LILY...

Tia stared anxiously at her daughter. 'Is she OK? She seems tiny—'

'Not that tiny for a thirty-four weeker,' Julie, the paediatrician, took the baby away for a quick examination and Luca prowled over to her side, watching every move she made.

'Are her lungs all right?'

His dark gaze was acute as he gazed down at his daughter, waiting impatiently while the paediatrician examined her.

'Everything seems fine at the moment,' Julie assured him, wrapping the baby carefully in warm blankets. 'Obviously we'll need to watch her carefully and see how she copes.'

'I've found the problem,' Dan said as he delivered the placenta. 'A small section had started to peel away. It's a good job we operated or this could have caused us a major problem later.'

Luca strode over to Dan's side and the two men spoke softly together as they looked at the placenta.

Finally Luca turned and returned to his seat by Tia's side, his eyes strained. 'You are feeling all right, *cara*?'

Tia nodded, exhausted but relieved that it was all over. 'Now what happens?'

'You go into the recovery room and get to know Lily, and after a bit we'll take you to the ward,' Polly told her, finishing off the swab count with Dan.

Tia lay there, gazing at her daughter, oblivious to the action still going on around her.

Finally they finished and she was wheeled through to the recovery room.

'We need to give her something to eat,' Polly said, gathering the charts together. 'Are you going to breastfeed her, Tia?'

Tia nodded. 'I want to.'

'OK, well, let's see if we can get her to latch on.' Polly positioned herself by the side of the trolley and together they tried to persuade Lily to feed. 'Your milk might not come in for a few days, but I don't need to tell you how good for her the colostrum is.'

Despite both their efforts, they had no success.

'She's not doing it.' Tia's voice was choked and Luca gave a frown.

'Give her a chance, Tia,' he said gently. 'She's tiny, *cara mia*. It takes a while to get the hang of it and she is only just thirty-four weeks. Her suck reflex may not have developed fully yet.'

They carried on trying and then Polly tested the baby's blood sugar. 'It's very low, Tia,' she said quietly. 'We really do need to get something into her. Can I give her a bottle for now?'

Tia nodded reluctantly, disappointed that she hadn't managed to breastfeed her daughter straight away but understanding that the important thing was that the baby had a feed of some kind because she was so tiny.

But Lily wouldn't take the bottle either and there was something else that was disturbing Luca.

'She's grunting,' he muttered, glancing across at Polly who nodded agreement.

Tia's heart fluttered in her chest. She knew that grunting was often the first sign of respiratory distress.

'But I thought her lungs were all right.' She turned to Luca, visibly upset, and he gave her shoulder a squeeze.

'She doesn't seem to be as well as we first thought,' he admitted, his voice rough with tension. 'She obviously hasn't developed her suck reflex yet and she's going to need some help with her breathing. She needs to go to Special Care for the time being, Tia.' He strode across to the phone and spoke to the paediatricians.

Tia looked at Polly with horror. 'But I don't want her to go to Special Care. I want her to stay here with me.'

Polly's eyes were sympathetic. 'I know that, Tia, but she needs some help. As soon as they've settled her you can go and visit her. We'll push you in the wheelchair.'

'Will you stay with her?' Tia turned to Luca, upset that she couldn't keep Lily with her.

'Of course.' Luca bent down and kissed her forehead. 'Don't worry.'

He scooped their daughter up gently and laid her carefully on his shoulder. 'I'll take her up myself, Polly. You stay with Tia.'

Polly frowned. 'I ought to ask them to bring down an incubator.'

'I would rather get her up there fast.' Without further conversation, Luca left the room and Tia watched them, totally unaware that Polly was talking to her.

'Tia?' Polly finished checking her friend's pulse and blood pressure and frowned down at her. 'I asked if you were in any pain.'

Pain?

'No.' And anyway she didn't care about pain. She just wanted her daughter to be OK.

By the time Luca reappeared Tia had been moved to the ward and settled in a bed.

After a conversation with Sharon, who was now back on duty, she'd persuaded the staff to remove her drip and her catheter.

'I want to be mobile as soon as possible,' she said stubbornly.

Dan popped up to see her and checked on the wound and her uterus and asked about her back.

'It aches a bit,' Tia admitted, 'but I know that's perfectly normal so you don't need to reassure me.'

Dan grinned. 'Having a well-informed patient is a mixed blessing. How's Lily?'

Tia tried to hide her anxiety but failed dismally. 'I don't know. Luca's been up there for ages…'

At that moment Luça walked quietly into the room, obviously expecting her to be asleep.

'Is she all right?' Tia winced as she struggled to sit upright and Luca frowned.

'You are in pain?'

'No,' Tia lied. 'How is Lily? What have they done? Is she ventilated?'

Luca sat down next to the bed and dealt with the questions one at a time. 'Overall, she's doing all right,' he said carefully, and Tia's breathing quickened.

'But she's got plenty wrong with her, hasn't she? I can tell that you're hiding something from me.' Her eyes filled. 'I want you to tell me the truth, Luca.'

'I'm not hiding anything.' He took her hand and gave her a tired smile. 'She's just very small and 34 weeks is a bit borderline, as you know. Some 34-weekers are perfectly capable of managing on their own without help and they do fine. Others need help.'

'How much help? Is she being ventilated?'

Tia knew from her own experience as a midwife that plenty of babies born prematurely needed ventilating to assist their breathing. Was this what had happened to little Lily?

Luca took a deep breath. 'You know she was grunting and you know as well as I do that that can be a sign of respiratory distress. She's also got a degree of intercostal recession and mild cyanosis. They're giving her CPAP.'

Tia stared at him, aware that with CPAP—continuous positive airways pressure—the baby was able to breathe independently but a continuous distending pressure was exerted on the airway to prevent the tiny air sacs in the lungs collapsing at the end of each respiration.

'Are they measuring her oxygen saturation?'

Luca nodded. 'It's variable, but they assure me that we can expect that with a 34-weeker. They're giving her oxygen and they've passed a nasogastric tube so that they can feed her. Later on, if you have the energy, you could try and express some milk for her and they can put that down the tube. We don't want to waste all those precious antibodies and we need to start stimulating your milk supply if she isn't going to feed immediately.'

Tia nodded immediately. 'Shall I do that now?'

'No.' He gave a gentle smile and gently squeezed her hand. 'You need some rest. How are you feeling? I want an honest answer.'

'I'm fine. I just want to get out of bed and go and see her.' Tia looked longingly at the wheelchair. 'Will you take me?'

'Now?' Luca glanced at Dan who shrugged.

'I don't see why not. She's not going to get any rest while she's worrying like this. Take her up there if she feels up to it.'

'All right.' Luca nodded slowly. 'But you need to have some more pain relief first.'

'Are you kidding?' Tia managed a wry smile as she got ready to transfer herself into the wheelchair. 'After labour pains, this is a piece of cake.'

Luca didn't smile. 'You know the rule, Tia. You have pain relief before the pain comes back and then it's easier to control it. You don't wait until you're in agony.'

Tia looked at him curiously. 'Why are you so worried about me being in pain? I'm fine, Luca, honestly.'

Luca let out a sharp breath. 'It was hell seeing you in so much pain when you were in labour,' he confessed quietly, and then surprised her by scooping her up easily into his arms and plopping her in the wheelchair as if she weighed nothing. 'I am very relieved that it is all over.'

She stared up at him, surprised by the strength of his reaction. She hadn't realised until now just how worried he'd obviously been. 'Will she be all right, Luca?'

'Tia, the girl has the entire paediatric department hovering over her,' he said dryly. 'Like you, I wish she was tucked up in here with us, but I'm not worried about her. Not at all.'

Tia started to relax for the first time in days. If Luca wasn't worried maybe there was no need for her to worry either.

She expressed some colostrum in the little room on Special Care and would have spent all day with Lily had Luca not forced her back downstairs to her room for a sleep.

'You will not help her if you collapse,' he pointed out roughly as he helped her back onto the bed.

Tia nodded and stifled a yawn, suddenly feeling more weary than she ever had in her life. She'd had a major operation, of course, so it was hardly surprising, and the strain of seeing their tiny daughter lying in an incubator connected to what seemed like hundreds of tubes was beginning to wear her down.

Luca looked as immaculate as ever but she could see from the fine lines around his dark eyes that he, too, was feeling the pressure.

She was all too aware that, despite his own personal worries, he'd concentrated all his attention on supporting her and overseeing the treatment their daughter was receiving. She loved him so much that it was a physical ache in her heart. Maybe it was time to tell him, she thought as sleep clouded her brain. Maybe it didn't matter that he didn't love her in the same way.

Tia slept on and off throughout the rest of the day, aware that Luca was dividing his time between her room and the special care baby unit where their daughter was being cared for.

Sharon helped her express more colostrum and then pushed her upstairs in the wheelchair so that she could feed it to Lily down the tube.

'Weird sort of breastfeeding, I know, sweetheart,' Tia murmured as she fiddled with the syringe and watched her tiny daughter smack her lips. 'Hurry up and learn to suck and then we can stop all this messing around.'

'We'll still put her to the breast regularly,' Sharon said, 'but don't forget that she's only tiny and she'll get tired easily.'

Tia looked at the baby wistfully. 'Do you think she'll ever breastfeed properly?'

'Oh, yes.' Sharon was adamant. 'If you really want to, I'm sure you'll manage it.'

Eventually Tia allowed herself to be wheeled back down to the ward for some more rest.

The next day was frantic with activity and both Dan and Duncan visited her to check that she was doing well physically. Despite the pain nagging in her wound, she was determined to be as mobile as possible to limit the possibility of clots forming in her legs.

Lily's condition seemed to fluctuate although no one seemed to be concerned that her problems were anything other than something to be expected in a baby of her gestation.

'When will I be able to take her home?' Tia asked the paediatric registrar and Julie gave a noncommittal shrug.

'You know better than anyone that I can't really answer that. The official answer at this stage is that she could be in until she should have been born—in other words, another six weeks—but I hope it won't be as long as that.'

Tia sagged with disappointment.

Six weeks?

Six weeks until they could take Lily home and start to be a family?

She spent most of the day with Lily, and Luca joined her periodically, dividing his time between his new family and his busy job.

'I've spoken to Dan and he's agreed that I can take two weeks off when Lily comes home,' he told her in a husky voice as they both leaned over the incubator.

Tia smiled up at him. Two weeks together? 'That's fantastic. How did you manage to persuade him to let you do that?'

'Threats mostly,' Luca admitted with a grin that melted her insides.

'I can't wait to go home,' she said softly, and his eyes locked onto hers.

'Me, too.' He hesitated and his smile faded. 'There is something I need to talk to you about. Something I should have said to you a long time ago.'

Tia felt as though she'd been showered with cold water.

Was he going to talk about Luisa? Now, after all this time?

Now that the baby was here, was he going to decide that their relationship was over?

Surely not. He adored Lily as much as she did.

But maybe he just wanted to be with Lily and not with her…

Hiding her panic, she concentrated her attention on the baby and barely noticed when Luca excused himself to answer his bleeper.

She barely saw him for the rest of the day and when she finally went to bed her mind was still tormented by worry and she couldn't settle.

Finally giving up on sleep, she glanced at the clock by her bed and saw that it was still only two o'clock in the morning.

Facing the fact that she wasn't going to get to sleep when

she was this worried about Luca, she decided to pay an impromptu visit to Lily. Tucking her feet into her slippers, she told the midwife in charge where she was going and walked gingerly to the lift.

She was managing to get around very well, although her wound still nagged painfully at times.

The lift moved silently upwards and the doors opened with a clatter that was magnified by the strange silence of the night.

The lights in the SCBU had been dimmed and Tia stopped to wash her hands and then walked onto the unit.

She stopped dead, surprised to see that Luca was there, his broad-shouldered figure bending over their daughter's cot.

And by his side was a tall, elegant, dark-haired woman whom she recognised in an instant. It was the same woman she'd seen talking to his mother on the day of the wedding.

Luisa.

Even as she watched in mute horror, he slipped an arm around the woman's shoulders and bent to drop a tender kiss on her forehead.

Dear God, no!

With a whimper of denial, Tia turned and shuffled from the room as fast as she could, determined to get back to the sanctuary of the ward before she collapsed.

Because collapse she would. She was only too painfully aware of that.

How could she have been such a fool?

She'd known all along that he had a secret, that he'd been involved with Luisa, but the truth was that she'd fallen so deeply in love with the man that she'd allowed herself to trust him.

But now that the baby had been safely born, he clearly wanted to be with the woman he loved.

And that woman was Luisa.

She was lying on the bed, tears pouring down her face, when the door opened and Luca walked in.

He gave a sharp exclamation when he saw that she was crying and was by her side in an instant.

'What's the matter?' His Italian accent was suddenly very pronounced. 'Are you in pain? Or is it hormones?'

Hormones?

Why was it that men were so quick to assume that when a woman was in tears it was caused by hormones?

He put out a hand to touch her but she flinched away from him and he frowned, clearly puzzled.

'Cara.'

'Don't call me that!' Her eyes filled again as she glared up at him. 'Our whole relationship is a total farce, Luca!'

He stilled, his expression shocked. 'Tia, you don't—'

'I am such a stupid fool,' she muttered, interrupting him without thought, rubbing the tears away from her cheeks with the palm of her hand. 'For a brief, totally deluded time, I really thought it could work between us.'

He frowned. 'Tia—'

'I was waiting for you to tell me, Luca.' She stared at him accusingly and reached for a tissue from the box by her bed. 'I wanted to see whether you were the same sort of man as my father.'

He was very still. 'Your father?'

'I told you that he had affairs,' Tia said hoarsely, 'but I never told you how my mother found out, did I? She fell down some stairs backstage and was unconscious in hospital for a week. My father really thought she was going to die so do you know what he did?' Her eyes were bright with tears of outrage as she looked at him. 'He chose that moment to confess everything. My mother was lying unconscious and he told her everything. All about the other women he'd been seeing—that their whole relationship had been a sham. He thought that she couldn't hear him, but she could.'

Luca's expression was grim. 'Tia, you don't—'

'She trusted him, you see,' Tia went on, her heart beating so fast she thought it would burst. 'And to find out that he had this secret life was just too much for her. When I heard your mother talking to Luisa the day of our wedding, it was like history repeating itself.'

There was a long silence and when he spoke his voice was soft. 'You heard my mother and Luisa talking?'

'That's right.' Tia nodded miserably, the words etched in her memory. 'Your mother said that it was a very sad day. That you were marrying the wrong woman for the wrong reasons and that you should have been marrying Luisa.' The tears started to trickle down her cheeks again and this time she did nothing to stop them. 'And then Luisa said that you'd told her that you would always love her. Which was all news to me, of course. Bad news. I was crazy about you, Luca. I really thought you were Mr Right.'

Luca's breathing was rapid and his face was dark with anger. 'Wait there,' he growled, turning on his heel and leaving the room, to return only minutes later, dragging Luisa by the arm.

He pushed her none too gently into the room and spoke to her rapidly in Italian, his expression grim.

Luisa listened and then glanced nervously at Tia. 'This is all my fault. Luca wants me to explain.'

'Don't bother,' Tia mumbled, reaching for another tissue and blowing her nose hard. 'I really don't want to hear it. I should have ended it the day of the wedding when I found out that that the pair of you were involved.'

Luisa's face blanched. 'That was why you refused to marry him? Because you thought that I, that we—?' She broke off and said something in Italian to Luca who shrugged, his eyes as hard as granite.

Strange, Tia thought dully as she tucked the scrunched tissue up her sleeve. For a man in love, he didn't look too happy.

'Tia…' Luisa's voice was suddenly shaking with nerves and she looked pleadingly at Luca who was totally unsympathetic. The Italian girl took a deep breath. 'I think… It seems as though you may have misunderstood—'

Luca growled something and she flinched slightly.

'I mean…' She cleared her throat and tried again. 'I was— I'm not involved with Luca. I never have been. Not in the way you imagined. But I wanted to be. I had a huge crush on him.'

She hung her head and Tia stared at her, uncomprehending. *A crush?*

'But I heard you and his mother talking. She said that he should be marrying you. You said that he'd promised to love you for ever.'

Luisa nodded. 'It's true that Luca's mother always wanted him to marry me, but it wasn't a realistic wish and it wasn't Luca's wish.' She bit her lip. 'The truth is that Luca was kind to me, always, and I—I wished it would be something more.'

'But it never was,' Luca said, speaking in English for the first time since he'd strode into the room, dragging Luisa with him. 'Luisa was a childhood friend of my sister's. My mother, who doesn't have enough to occupy her mind, weaved all sorts of plans for bringing us together. But they didn't work.'

Hope started to flicker in the back of Tia's mind. 'They didn't?'

'No.' Luca looked at Luisa and gave her a crooked smile, the sort that a brother might have given to a sister. 'Whenever Luisa and I went out, it was always with the family. We were never involved in a romantic sense.'

Tia swallowed. 'But you told her that you'd always love her.'

Luca frowned. 'I may have told her that, but—'

'But he didn't mean it in a romantic sense.' Luisa spoke in a pathetically small voice. 'When I found out he was marrying you I went to see him at the hospital and—well, he was kind to me but very blunt. He told me again that he would never want a relationship with me. I was dreadfully upset and he did tell me that he'd always love me, but of course he just meant as a friend. Deep down I knew there was no hope, but I had a terrible crush on him. I was still kidding myself that he loved me when I spoke to his mother the day of your wedding. I was so crazy about him it made me do stupid things—do you understand?'

Tia thought she probably did understand. She knew just how powerful an effect Luca could have on women.

'So you're saying…' Her voice cracked and she looked at Luca questioningly. 'You're saying that what I heard the day of the wedding was nonsense?'

'Complete nonsense.' Luca's eyes gleamed. 'Something I would have confirmed had you bothered to ask me. Next time you overhear something, it might be wise to discuss it with me, *cara mia*. It might save us all a great deal of anguish.'

Tia glanced back at Luisa. 'So why have you come here now?'

Luisa blushed. 'I've met someone,' she confessed, 'and we are on holiday in England. I wanted to bring him to meet Luca and apologise for my behaviour. I threw myself at him and behaved very badly.'

Tia flopped back against her pillows and stared at Luca, the colour rising in her cheeks as she met his eyes.

'Luisa, I believe your boyfriend is waiting downstairs.' Luca barely gave her a glance but she took the hint immediately.

'Yes, I've got to go.' She hurried towards the door and cast a final apologetic look at Tia before leaving the room.

Tia stared down at the bedcovers, not knowing what to say. She felt the bed dip and Luca's solid thigh appeared in her line of vision.

'Luca, I'm sorry,' she whispered, hardly daring to look

at him. 'I ruined the wedding and…I really thought yo⟨u⟩ were in love.'

'I was in love,' he said quietly, reaching for her hand⟨s⟩ and taking them in his. 'With you. From the first momen⟨t⟩ I saw you in Venice.'

She lifted her eyes to his and shook her head slightly⟨.⟩ 'No.'

'Yes,' he said firmly.

There was a long silence. A silence that seemed to stretc⟨h⟩ for ever.

Finally Tia shifted. 'But—'

'It seems to me that we still aren't talking enough, *cara*,⟨'⟩ he murmured, his voice rough as he stroked her cheek wit⟨h⟩ the back of his hand. 'So I'm going to talk now. It's tru⟨e⟩ that Luisa had a crush on me and maybe I should have tol⟨d⟩ you, but to be honest it didn't seem important. I was i⟨n⟩ love with you and spending all my time trying to find way⟨s⟩ to make you love me back. I thought that when I told m⟨y⟩ family I was getting married the problem of Luisa woul⟨d⟩ be solved.'

Tia stared at him. 'But I thought you were marrying m⟨e⟩ because I was pregnant.'

He shook his head slowly. 'No. I was marrying you be-cause I was in love with you. Madly in love with you.'

'But when I told you that I was pregnant, you were hor-rified.'

He sighed and ran a hand through his hair. 'I know tha⟨t⟩ it seemed that way, but it wasn't true. I was very pleased⟨,⟩ but also very afraid.'

'Afraid?' She was thoroughly confused and he gave ⟨a⟩ sigh.

'Yes, afraid. You see, I knew how wary you were o⟨f⟩ men,' he said quietly. 'I knew that you were very confused⟨,⟩ about your feelings for me. I could see that what happened between us physically confused and overwhelmed you, and

I was trying to give you space and time to adjust. And then we found out that you were pregnant.'

'I thought you didn't want me any more. You spent more and more time at the hospital.'

'That's true.' His voice was suddenly gruff and he walked slowly back to the bed and settled himself next to her. 'And the reason I spent all that time at the hospital was because I was desperate to finish writing up my research work so that I could be released early and take a job in England. I wanted to take you home, Tia. I thought things might be easier between us if you were in your own country.'

Her eyes met his, her heart thumping uncomfortably in her chest. What was he saying?

'I loved you from the first moment I saw you. But before you had time to get used to the idea you were pregnant, and I was so angry with myself for that. You were so wary of marriage, I should have given you time to adjust to the idea, instead of which I moved so fast you barely had time to think. And then you panicked. You were suddenly terrified of what you'd done, totally overwhelmed by the enormity of it. And I knew that I'd made a mistake to rush you.'

Tia nodded warily. 'How did you know that?'

'I could read your body language,' he said softly. 'Our sex life was as miraculous as ever but the rest of the time you were restless and unsettled. I was cursing myself for not being more restrained that first night together. I should have taken it slowly but at the time all I could think about was making you mine. I knew from the first moment I saw you that you were the only woman I wanted to spend my life with.'

Tia could hardly believe what she was hearing. *The only woman he wanted to spend his life with?*

'Really?'

'Really,' he said softly, a strange light in his dark eyes.

'And I thought that you felt the same way, which was why I had no conscience about rushing you into marrying me On the day of the wedding, when I discovered that you' gone…' He closed his eyes briefly. 'Well, let's just say tha it was the worst day of my life.'

Tia was stunned. 'But you never told me that. You neve told me that you loved me.'

'Because I didn't want to put more pressure on you,' h said. 'And I suppose because I'd never actually said those words to any woman and I found it difficult to say them.'

'I didn't know,' Tia said. 'I thought that you didn't love me.'

He closed his eyes and shook his head. 'Tia, everyone knows I'm crazy about you, except you. Sharon, Duncan even Dan because I'd forgotten that he spoke reasonabl Italian when I told you exactly how I felt in Theatre the other night.'

Tia stared at him in wonder. 'You told me that you loved me?'

He gave a crooked smile. 'And a few other soppy thing: that Dan obviously understood very clearly—I must re member to ask him where he acquired his knowledge o Italian.' He touched her cheek with gentle fingers. 'What a pair of fools we have been. When I discovered that you had left, I almost lost my sanity. I assumed that the baby had been the final straw and you had left in a panic.'

'But when you turned up in England, you still didn't tel me you loved me,' Tia pointed out. 'You said that we owed it to the baby to make our relationship work—'

'You seemed so determined to give up on what we had,' he said quietly. 'I used the baby to buy myself more time Time to convince you that what we had was unique.'

Tia felt suddenly shy. 'And then you agreed to all my terms and conditions.'

'Of course.' He gave a wry smile. 'I would have agreed to anything to keep you by my side.'

She gave a little smile. 'You even stopped complaining about me working.'

He nodded slowly, his expression suddenly serious. 'I understand now why you feel such a strong need to work. It is understandable after such an awful childhood. You need to feel secure. But, Tia, you can trust me. I don't mind if you want to work but I need you to know that I will always be here to look after you.'

'I know that. I love you, Luca,' she whispered softly. 'I always have.'

He gave a groan and scooped her into his arms, kissing her gently on the mouth.

'Will you forgive me for rushing you? For doing everything back to front?' He murmured the words against her mouth, his hands sliding gently over her shoulders. 'I seduced you that first night without giving you time to get to know me. But I always knew you were the only woman for me.'

Tia pulled away from him, her eyes teasing. 'And what about all these other women that drool over you? What are we going to do about them?'

Luca's eyes gleamed. 'I'm not interested, *cara*, you should know that by now. There is only one other woman who will ever claim my attention.'

Tia stiffened and then she saw the light dancing in his wicked dark eyes and she smiled.

'Lily.'

'Lily.' He repeated their daughter's name softly. 'Already she is turning my heart and my life upside down, exactly like her mother.'

The look in his eyes melted Tia's insides. 'I love you, Luca.'

He murmured in Italian and bent his head to kiss her. 'And I love you, too, *cara mia*. For ever.'

EPILOGUE

'IF YOU break the zip on this dress I'll kill you.' Sharon stood back and admired her handiwork, her expression softening as she looked at her friend. 'You look beautiful and you're a lucky girl, do you know that?'

'Yes.' Tia walked across the room to the Moses basket where Lily lay fast asleep.

She *was* incredibly lucky.

'And this hotel is fabulous,' Sharon observed, glancing out of the window towards the large ornamental lake. 'I'll say this for him, Luca certainly isn't stingy. All right. We're due downstairs. The guests are waiting, and this time we're not giving them a fright.'

Tia smiled and bent to pick up the basket. 'She can stay at the back of the room with you until we've finished.'

But Lily had other ideas.

The minute Tia picked up the basket she started to howl and Tia gave a groan of disbelief.

'No! Not now, Lily. You can't be hungry yet.'

'Just get downstairs,' Sharon said quickly. 'I'll keep her happy until you're ready.'

Tia looked at her daughter and her heart twisted. She was so tiny and helpless and she'd only been out of hospital for three weeks.

'I can't.' She shook her head firmly. 'Not if she needs feeding. I'll feed her and then I'll get married.'

Sharon looked frantically at the clock. 'Tia, you can't do this again! Luca will have a nervous breakdown.'

'Except that this time I'm leaving nothing to chance.' Luca's deep drawl came from the doorway and he walked

184

over to Tia, his expression faintly mocking. 'Leaving me waiting at the altar again, *cara mia*?'

'Luca!' Sharon's voice was a horrified squeak. 'You're not meant to see the bride before you marry her.'

Luca smiled. 'I don't care what she's wearing as long as she turns up.'

Tia looked at him anxiously. 'Lily's hungry.'

'Then feed her,' Luca said softly, removing his jacket and tossing it carelessly onto the bed. 'Otherwise you will worry and I don't want you to worry. I want this to be a day you remember.'

Ignoring Sharon's anxious mutterings about the time, Tia allowed Luca to unzip her dress and settled herself in the chair to feed the baby.

'I don't believe this.' Sharon's expression was comical as she looked at them. 'You know that they're all going to think that you've done it again.'

Tia looked at Luca but he simply shrugged.

'We don't care what people think,' he reminded her lightly. 'They will wait, *cara mia*. Sharon, if it bothers you so much, go down and tell them that we are feeding Lily and will join them in a moment.'

Sharon looked from one to the other and gave a sigh. 'Maybe I'll do that.'

She left the room, closing the door quietly behind her.

Luca stroked Tia's cheek with a gentle finger. 'I thought you had changed your mind again,' he admitted gruffly, and Tia shook her head, her eyes soft with love.

'Never. But Lily started to cry.'

He gave a chuckle. 'I told you that you would be a good mother.'

'I love her, Luca,' Tia said in a choked voice, handing him the baby as she rearranged her dress and got unsteadily to her feet.

'I know you do.' He transferred the baby to his shoulder

and bent to kiss Tia gently on the mouth. 'And she is a lucky girl to have you as a mother.'

Tia gave him a shy smile. 'I still can't believe we're going to be a proper family.'

'Well, we are.' Luca held his daughter snugly with one arm and retrieved his jacket with the other. 'Are you ready to marry me?'

Tia nodded slowly. Oh, yes, she was ready. She was more than ready.

He smiled and held out his free hand. 'So do you think we should get a move on before we give our guests a heart attack for a second time?'

Tia slipped her hand into his and her eyes twinkled into his. 'I do...'

The world's bestselling romance series.

HARLEQUIN®
Presents

Seduction and Passion Guaranteed!

Legally wed, great together in bed,
but he's never said…"I love you."

They're…

Wedlocked!

The series
in which
marriages are
made in haste…
and love
comes later…

Don't miss

THE TOKEN WIFE by Sara Craven,
#2369 on sale January 2004

Coming soon

THE CONSTANTIN MARRIAGE by Lindsay Armstrong,
#2384 on sale March 2004

Pick up a Harlequin Presents® novel and you will
enter a world of spine-tingling passion and
provocative, tantalizing romance!

Available wherever Harlequin books are sold.

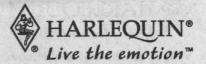

HARLEQUIN®
Live the emotion™

Visit us at www.eHarlequin.com

HPWEDJF

The world's bestselling romance series.

HARLEQUIN®
Presents

Seduction and Passion Guaranteed!

INTERNATIONAL
DOCTORS

They're guaranteed to raise your pulse!

**Meet the most eligible medical men of the world,
in a new series of stories, by popular authors,
that will make your heart race!**

**Whether they're saving lives or dealing with desire,
our doctors have got bedside manners that
send temperatures soaring....**

Coming in Harlequin Presents in 2003:

THE DOCTOR'S SECRET CHILD by Catherine Spencer
#2311, on sale March

THE PASSION TREATMENT by Kim Lawrence
#2330, on sale June

THE DOCTOR'S RUNAWAY BRIDE by Sarah Morgan
#2366, on sale December

**Pick up a Harlequin Presents® novel and you will enter a world
of spine-tingling passion and provocative, tantalizing romance!**
Available wherever Harlequin books are sold.

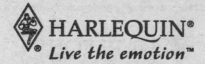

HARLEQUIN®
Live the emotion™

Visit us at www.eHarlequin.com

HPINTDOC

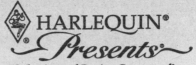

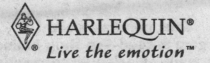

If you enjoyed what you just read,
then we've got an offer you can't resist!

Take 2 bestselling love stories FREE!

Plus get a FREE surprise gift!

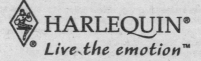